ponyboy

ponyboy

a novel

Eliot Duncan

W. W. NORTON & COMPANY
Celebrating a Century of Independent Publishing

For information about permission to reproduce selections from this book,
write to Permissions, W. W. Norton & Company, Inc.,
500 Fifth Avenue, New York, NY 10110

For information about special discounts for bulk purchases, please contact
W. W. Norton Special Sales at specialsales@wwnorton.com or 800-233-4830

Manufacturing by Lakeside Book Company
Book design by Chris Welch
Production manager: Lauren Abbate

ISBN 978-1-324-05122-0 (pbk)

W. W. Norton & Company, Inc., 500 Fifth Avenue, New York, N.Y. 10110
www.wwnorton.com

W. W. Norton & Company Ltd., 15 Carlisle Street, London W1D 3BS

1 2 3 4 5 6 7 8 9 0

to all the boys who were first girls

Author's Note

Although some of this novel was inspired by my life, this is a work of fiction and the usual rules apply. All characters, events and incidents have been fictionalized and reflect my imagination, and none should be understood as a literal depiction of any person, event or incident.

negative three:
birth in verse

Toni, Paris

Toni sweeps my hair off the gray bathroom tile and asks, Do you know what it feels like to *really* make eye contact with yourself? The tiny flecks make my neck and shoulders itch. I try and fail at brushing them off. I meet my inescapable form in the mirror, find Toni's gaze and shrug. My eyes seem bigger. My jaw, more structural.

Toni's acrylics are goth elegance: a blue close to black, each nail filed to a point. They run down my newly buzzed skull. Tiny, cold waves slosh down my spine. I smile, calmed by Toni's touch. I breathe there for a second, then scan down my torso. It doesn't make sense. I press down on my chest. I've always known that they're fundamentally pec muscle. I cringe at their indecent bounce and certain weight, the impossibility of hiding them. An inevitable symbol for recognition out in the world, my life sentence as woman, girl.

I saved a six-pack all day, a great accomplishment. Now I gulp deep. Chilly, golden bubbles in my chest. My binder makes chugging hard. You're not supposed to smoke with it on, says the internet. Each beer tilt on my lips crashes through my entire body—bringing ease, then, later, a smothering oblivion.

I want to make eye contact with myself. I stand on the couch and look for me in the cracked mirror over the fireplace. Light a cig. Turn horizontal. The curve of my chest flattened but not gone. No. They're, visually, slightly there. Still, the binder's heavy compression allows me to move, to assert my boyhood with less fear.

Toni reads something thick in the chair across from me. They've tied up their long dark hair, and there's a golden shimmer on their eyelids. We catch each other's glances and they begin cutting lines on the coffee table. Their hands are quick, elegant truths and I want to tell them so. Instead, I take the line they sliced for me and kiss the heaven of their neck.

Toni smells like before. We grew up and over and out of Iowa, together. After high school Toni went to Providence and me, here, to Paris. I move freer in their company, in the comfort and simultaneous ache of knowing someone so well for so long. More and more, they show me I could exist, that I could live. They allow the light of me to come forth, giving grace to even the shame of me. My truth able to arise, unmuffled and frank. It's not *your* shame, they'd say, it doesn't belong to you. Never has.

My girlfriend, Baby, left Paris for a couple weeks to make art in Hackney with her hot mentor and professor, Sophia. Not knowing how to be alone more than I already always was, I begged Toni to come see me. When I picked them up at Charles de Gaulle, they looked different: softer, glowy. In their long hug, my everything stirred.

Without Baby my living room is sterile, especially for a Saturday. Toni and I will go out tonight or people will come here and we'll laugh and dance and sure, there will be rants, and maybe we'll fuck. I smell greatness all around my life. Maybe that's cocaine. My movements are welding into a smoother, masculine strut. My cock-intelligence smolders in my furrowed brow. Sharp clusters of percussion move me. I move more now than ever. I've got a whole world erupting outside the one that they spun on woman orbit. A whole world to let go of from white-knuckled grip. I have to get rid. Have to let it fall. I finish my beer. Start another. And another. The Misfits, I think. Just more Misfits.

Toni keeps their estrogen pills in a small golden tin, a heart etched on the top. I accidentally brush the tin off the coffee table on my swoop out of the apartment. We crouch, picking up the flat green ovals. They put their hand out for the pills I've collected, laughing. Unable to feel anything but thirst, I tell them: I'm just gonna duck out for some beer.

At the alimentation générale, I slide one green bottle into the front of my tight, overdyed Wranglers. The cold bottle rests between my skin and a copy of *Leash* by Jane Delynn, a parting gift from Baby. I'll never finish it. It makes me too hard. Still, I keep it close to me wherever I go. I pull it out from time to time, sighing into a line on the métro, in a café, at the bar. I dream with its paragraphs, feeling Baby beside me.

I tie my thick denim jacket around my hips. I grab four more bottles and walk wide to the counter. Without thought, I ask for two bottles of whiskey.

I hear Baby go: Really? But she's not here for a whiskey

limit, not here to touch the back of my neck, not here to demand wide angles of time from me, not here to look up at me when she's down on me—her enormous brown eyes, her mouth and long fingers not here to erode me.

The guy at the counter smiles. Baby told me that this guy knows I steal. Then why doesn't he say something? Maybe he finds your childish theft charming, she said. I wink at the guy. I pay and leave with Baby hot in my mind.

Rue Saint-Denis shudders inside me: the clogged corners I swivel past, with women waiting in tight colors and thin-strapped sandals, men in blazers, people yelling out prices of fruit arranged in pyramids, wet vegetables and laid-out fish. The pigeons are in one shitty flock under the arc, La Porte Saint-Denis. Then there's the piss stench, the cigarette—perpetual and essential. Some people, part of another world, eat on sunny terraces at cafés. They're clean, aloof. Lovingly, I navigate this ancient city's crevices. I dodge lingering eyes. My core expands into the street. I touch everything with my heart. I give the guy outside the tabac a couple cigs and light one for myself. A group of people pass with rolled canvas and violet fabric under their arms. A man without a shirt jogs down the middle of the road and I vanish into envy for his flat chest.

July's heat is amplified: it smacks limestone, cobblestone, then limestone again. We humans get damp, rude and slow. Past a short tangle of bikes and cars, light posts and leafy trees is my door. It's painted a worn but vivid Grecian blue. The narrow front corridor is dark. It has a bank of mailboxes. Bikes and strollers lean on the adjacent mirror. I take a hard right and walk up to the hot cube of my apartment. Seven flights. No thin, slow elevator. Just me taking every other step, wings tucked, whiskey close.

My space is eighteen square meters, large for a chambre de bonne. It's on the very top floor, which, in Hausmannian buildings, were the maid's quarters. The room has a full-sized bed, a small couch, a desk and a coffee table. Next to a built-in cabinet for clothes and an old fireplace are a mini-fridge, a sink, and a hot plate. The ceiling is a slanted wall, the underside of a mansard roof. There's one thick, exposed wooden beam, a spine. The single window on the slanted wall, when swung open, makes it possible to think. The bathroom, off the entry, has a porcelain tub and no showerhead. On the wall along the tub, where the tiles end, is a wobbly wooden shelf. I keep my hottest books there.

I hear music from the hallway and feel a shiver down my leg from the beer in my waistband. Toni greets me with their voracious grace: Ponyboy! They're railing through the blow and someone I don't know is on the couch looking prim and bothered. I meet her, a friend of Toni's from Brown. I feel nothing, pass her a beer. Toni takes one step to the kitchen, looking at what I bought. And this, I say with a smile, pulling the large green bottle from my jeans. Toni wants whiskey on ice. I remind Toni but mainly me: Take it easy, love. I briefly hold the place where their jaw and neck meet. My hand, pedestrian. They kiss the inside of my wrist. Cheers. They lift their drink. Cheers.

Toni gestures to their friend: We were just talking about somatic fictions. Cool, I say. With the heat, Toni's enthusiastic company irritates me. There's no space for me. I drink fast,

fast and then faster. I want to melt all over the room. I want to not be a body anymore. I want to slick warm and affectionately away from the self I was taught to be, sliding over their conversation and out the window, into mother evening.

Toni goes on, Remember when you said that you didn't know if you wanted to be a boy or be treated like one? I pour and down another drink, taking an ice cube to the back of my neck. I sit next to Toni's sweating friend on the couch. I respond, Your answer, Toni, was: What's the difference? Exactly! Toni snaps: Gendered ontologies are productive, categorical fictions. To be is the same as to be treated as. I say, To be treated as is to be? I don't know, Toni. I want to grab the red journal Baby gave me but it's been elected holding place for the tidy pile of drugs.

Toni's friend politely asks: I'm sorry, what's your name again? Not looking up, I shrug: What's yours? I'm Dover, she says, putting her cold beer on my cheek. I turn to her. Thanks, Dover, I whisper, letting her cold gesture become everything.

Just as I close my eyes, Toni tells me to come have a look at myself. I open my eyes and Dover takes her beer back to her mouth. I stand up slowly and look down at myself in the massive oval mirror laid on the coffee table. My face is sliced by Toni's cocaine spurs. Trying to really see myself among the white banks, I whisper: Ponyboy. Touching my forearm like she's my girlfriend, Toni nods: Ponyboy.

As Toni unpacked, they handed me their button-downs and blazers. I passed them my dresses, tank tops and skirts. On the night they arrived, they walked, jet-lagged, disheveled and stunning, around my tiny apartment, touching the slanted roof and exposed beam. They smiled: This is beautiful. Look outside, I said. We leaned out the open window, elbow to elbow, and laughed at their mom believing we were a hetero couple in high school. We really did punk everyone, Toni said, taking a bad photo of the street below.

Later, we sat on my bed and looked through old photos on Facebook. Toni drank coffee. I poured myself more red wine and calibrated how much blow was hidden in my desk.

With each click a smooth, heavy stone sank deeper into my core. I can totally see you as a boy in these, Toni said. Thank you. They laughed at a photo of me in a short black dress. My hair long and brown. Eyes far, far off somewhere. That was the night we snorted their sister's Adderall since the principal breathalyzed at the entrance. I remember taking off my impossible heels and staring at the gym floor as Toni lightly grinded with their calculus teacher.

As I stared at my nearly empty glass, I felt an ancient cry brew. Look at this one. Toni stopped at a photo of us in middle school. Black fluffy wings are strapped to their back. I'm in a black suit with an unlit cigar in my mouth, chin cocked high, eyes looking down. Mom, entertained, agreed to slick my hair back. What *was* I for Halloween? Yourself, Toni said with a laugh, and no one recognized you.

An Interlude of Becoming, House Party, American Midwest

I forgot to keep talking, that's the thing. I meant to look people in their eyes, I meant to ask for help. I meant to keep it all in check so that I didn't get lost again. That's what's true now: I'm lost again.

My body holds every stray gaze, every man's breath on my neck, forcing inside all their ache, all their hate for the world, for themselves. It's not just the living men, but those canonized, those held reverent too. Nietzsche's cock-consciousness looms at my door. I use his dead language as he shoves into me with violent genius, whispering: "Werde, der du bist."

My body holds that kind of projectile agony: one large living man at a party holding me down. I became a fish on his dock, swarming for the cool lake of ferment that I knew as home: another bottle of anything, *please* another drink. To extend the metaphor, I'd tell you I took his bait, but the conceit doesn't track. He pulled me out of the water bare-handed and the air was his, so I suffocated. I was fourteen, maybe fifteen, and all wide-eyed, unmoving, coming to. He hurt, fucking dreams and breath out of me forever.

Toni, Paris

Now my life droops on this hooked orbit. My central tug, mother alcohol, builds me rooms to live inside—ones I don't have to actually be inside to be inside. I lose my body exceptionally. I come to and know any stranger's touch as inevitable. With alcohol's force, I have words to say, thoughts to think.

I wake up with huge, glorious gaps from every evening prior. Parts come back to me in horrific, cinematic blasts. My feet jump off a dark green bench. Toni's gorgeous mind leads me. Then the next day, pacing around, eating bites of food, drinking mugs of coffee. Waiting for night, to drink and forget things again. I slither from bed, step in a puddle of beer. Toni's in the bathroom. "This Charming Man" loops. I clean up the spill with my/Dad's Dead Kennedys T-shirt and halfheartedly sing: "Will nature make a man of me yet?" What can I do with all this desire except go forward with it in my palms?

Baby, Paris

A week before Toni's visit, Baby woke branched in the crux of my arm. The morning was flat, blue and gray. I felt far away from each corner, every tilt, edge and crack of our apartment. The next day, she would leave for London with Sophia.

Will you email every day? Baby asked as she stepped out of bed. Sure. I nodded and swallowed, getting into my binder. The buzzer buzzed and Baby slid into jeans and a red sports bra. She jogged to the door. Oui? C'est moi.

It's Sophia. I know, I said, rolling my eyes, throwing on Baby's blue T-shirt and my black jeans. Baby looked at me from the door and asked if I'd choose the music. Mhmm. I moved to her, lifting her in my arms, her legs wrapped around my waist. The seven flights gave us time. I walked us to the couch, our hearts close, my breath on her neck. I'll miss you, I said.

Sophia knocked. Baby unraveled from me and went to the door to greet her. I put on a Townes Van Zandt record that made me think of Mom—the album with him sitting at a desk, the one with the blue door. I stepped to the kitchen and made us all coffee.

Sophia was wide-strided, an authority. At forty-six, she was more than twenty years ahead of us. She drove a red vintage Triumph. Her skin had been punctured with more ink; she had bathed in more seas. She'd loved more people, seen more of the sky. She'd been before we were. Rare, to see a life that proved the potential for our own. Most of the time, the future felt like an obscure projection I was afraid to want because there wasn't evidence of future me anywhere, in life or in fiction. I just knew Jack Halberstam and I were the same, so I existed there, in theory.

Sophia nodded at me in the open kitchen and sat on the couch. Her slanted smile hit cool, shy and untryingly alpha. Baby sat next to her and I watched them every few seconds while the coffee got strong, noting the proximity of their words.

I set down mugs of coffee between us. Tomorrow is the day, Sophia stated plainly, her hands on her knees: Ready for London? Baby nodded at the rolls of canvas in the corner. I sipped my coffee slow and looked out the window to the building across, at the slabs of limestone, the glossy windows in sun, the wrought-iron curvature. When I focused on Townes Van Zandt's pleading confidence, I felt the tall grass of Grandma's farm and her red truck on gravel.

Sophia asked how I'll survive two weeks without Baby. I don't know, I joked: I'll probably just kill myself. I knew with hilarity that the very thing keeping me alive, in orbit, was the same thing that could end me, that could fling me into a quiet, dark forever. Baby laughed like that was inevitable, but she knew like I knew: no matter how close to death I'd venture, I'd always come back for her. Sophia's silence filled the space with grounded concern. Townes Van Zandt kept it all heavy. Sophia sweetly tried, But you'll get a lot of reading done, no? I nod. An old friend, Toni, is coming to visit from the States.

A day later, I woke not knowing how I got back to my apartment. I opened the massive window on the slanted wall above my bed and smoked, looking at the street below. As I blinked into living, I remembered the Seine's silky black surface from a cab, a warmth, a strobe light, shots, a staircase, a touch from another and a bathroom stall. Getting gone like that had sunk into an average aspect of my life.

As I watched people filter in and out of the grocery store below, my phone rang. The screen said Mom. I answered reluctantly. I shaped my voice into someone else, Hey. Hey, sweetheart. I tell her this and that, moving books around, opening my empty fridge, and trying to make my bed. She asks about school and I tell her my philosophy degree is going well. As I look at the books I haven't read, I say I might want to stay for a year or two after graduating. I hadn't been doing well this last semester. I could barely make it to class. She asks me how often I see my dad. Every now and then, I assure her. Dad moved around a lot for work but had settled, more or less, with his partner in Germany. Mom and he divorced just before high school ended. I wanted to get far, far away, and when I asked, Dad agreed to support me and my studies in Paris.

Toni is coming tomorrow, I say. Remember Toni? She did.

She asked if we were building something romantic. I have a girlfriend, I reminded her. She told me she has a new boyfriend; they go bow hunting at Grandma's farm. She says elk is delicious. Oh—I stare far off somewhere—cool, that's very cool.

American Midwest

I'm cold, seventeen and drinking shit whiskey on a porch in Lincoln. Earlier, I promised a different version of myself I wouldn't finish the last bottle, let alone steal this one. I'm alone but gorgeous in this dismal, obsessional fight of every-day. I always surrender away from, not to. I'm on the porch of a house that could be any house on a street that could be any street.

Too-frequent, too-bright streetlights illuminate clusters of other drunk people. No one wears coats. I see girls with smoothed legs, small wallets tied to their wrists, looking like they piss rosewater. They're strong, I think, for having to be so cold and around so many entitled men at night.

I look back inside the house. People are yelling and laughing. I slam the glass of my dark, chemical heat and shiver. My/Dad's thick leather jacket is stiffened with December cold. The neighboring houses are tucked in darkness or else are lit with sound and people. I look at my drink, wanting something to happen.

My sister, looking too gorgeous for this town, brings me

the tallboys I asked for. She stumbles a little but sits next to me. She invited me and Mom to her college town, to celebrate her early graduation, a bachelor's degree in political science. I drape my/Dad's coat over her shoulders. She raises her drink, we cheers. Congrats on being done with high school, she tells me. I laugh. Thanks. She asks, Are you coming in? Men scream louder inside. Not yet. I bring a cig to my lips. The lighter takes a second—the fluid gone cold. My sister tells me she's going to take the LSAT. I know, I say, you're going to be a great lawyer. The alcohol has smoothed out her language, made it docile, blurry: You're going to be great, I mean, living in France, she said. With my index and middle on the top of the cig, my thumb under, I drag long and pull it down from the very middle of my lips. She asks, Why are you smoking like that? Like what? I ask, avoiding her corrective gaze. She says flatly: Like a boy.

A bare, remote stillness fell. Some bad of me had been revealed. I'd been found out. I surfaced a shallow smile, crossed my legs: What are you talking about? She took her index and fixed a smudge of the makeup I put on earlier. We looked to the street. It's too cold out here, she said. She swayed my/Dad's leather jacket off her shoulders and I put it back on. As she opened the front door, sticky pop and blown-out bass, blue light, sex, sugary alcohol and laughs spilled out. A shard of an actual me rose up with an unutterable clarity and then, was gone.

Baby, Paris

Baby and I met at a party. Someone said there'd be a performance piece, but it was just a bunch of queers getting fucked
up in a small apartment in the 3rd. A guy did tattoos in the
corner. She was laid on the couch, the guy needling something into her ankle. Her thick brow was furrowed and her
glasses were worn low on her nose. She had a long frame and
a bottle of white wine was on the floor below her. She took
lines offered by a friend. She was doing so many things at
once so well. I was amorous, silent. I decided to smoke by the
window and try to ignore her.

T'as un feu?

Ouais. I passed her my lighter. T'es française?

Non, je viens de Toronto, mais chui Brazilian.

Oh, I'm American, I said with regret.

She inhaled, the ember glowing good. I turned to look out
onto the street, to look where she looked. I heard there would
be a performance, I said. Ha. She rolled her eyes. It's a good
way to keep your guests interested, isn't it? I stood a little
taller, hoping my binder flattened me enough.

Her black jeans seemed lived-in, wiped with paint and plaster, resin, glue and clay. I got nervous. I said: You're wearing a manifesto. Unaffected, she looked down and said, Things just get messy. I nodded and saw sawdust lingering in her hair. Her eyes held hot planets. Her eyeliner smeared to black points. Cast in moonlight, her saffron wings grew with breath, more and less visible behind the slope of her neck and shoulders.

I saw her looking down at me with wings wide. I was getting hard and my eyes, sinking and focused, showed it. Dance music for sad people played. She asked my name. I shrugged. I asked about her new tattoo. She said it said flight. Then she twisted, hip up, to show me the back of her left thigh. With my freebased, blow-smeared cigarette relaxed on my lips, I bent down to look closer. Sewn into her jeans in urgent, jagged magenta was:

Não passarão.

Drugs bonded Baby and me. I didn't mean to love that about us but I did. All of a sudden getting totally fucked three nights a week became every night. She brought drugs deeper into my world and I couldn't let go. She could. Anytime she was over it, she'd just stop. She quit when she was feeling good. Her reserve was impressive to me and seemed like a rare fluke. No one really has control like that, I thought. To me, everyone was doing what I was doing and drugs were the only thing I was ever really doing.

When I didn't have a lecture or essay due, I was drunk by afternoon and speeding all night. Baby was with me anyway. She never actually tried to stop me. She'd indulge too, in her own way, so I never needed to flat-out hide or lie too large. Blow and speed amplified my life, letting me drink longer and think wilder.

What is ********poem************ but
************tufts of green in the crevices******* of that
sky*scraper*****************
*******no one looks like a boy to me anymore*************
*********** *******************my nail polish falls off **********in***
****

**********P***********E*******T****a********L*************************
*********S

We respected, with all our heft, one another's work. She'd read any line, any story, and give me thoughtful notes. She'd tell me to write more, that I had to. She gave me Cookie Mueller's book *Walking Through Clear Water in a Pool Painted Black*. I gave her my copy of Paul Preciado's *Testo Junkie* and she read it. She added notes to my notes in the margins.

I'd go to every exhibition days before with her, helping her install, looking long and hard at this placement over that, bringing her black tea and candy and beer and, at night, when the gallery was empty, I'd get hard and we'd kiss our way to the small kitchen.

Once, I carried her to face me on the yellow-tiled counter, her legs wrapped around me. Her grip would go from my neck to my chest, where I'd have to remind her: No. While she slipped out of her jeans, I'd situate myself. Her legs around me that way made me feel like a parenthetical, like I was hers. I'd find her eyes so that I could remind myself I could be, that I was, that I am.

Then she'd unzip my jeans and there I'd persist, hard. Kissing her neck, I'd follow her sounds. My hands on her thigh as I'd go, she'd look at me and I'd love deeper, making room for my self inside her. Her breath, urgent-beautiful and full.

She'd say secret dreams to me: Please, cum inside me. She'd call me Daddy. In our clothed lives, though, she was slow to call me boyfriend. She'd always insist that she wasn't straight, which left me shrugging: Neither am I. Which left her asking, Then what? Then everything, I'd think, then none and each. Then I'm a sky close to ocean, an ocean close to sky.

I'd nearly lose it but would go on filling her up. Then she'd release all chaotic and perfect. I'd stay inside her as our wings softened, my hand on her lower back, holding her up. I'd tell her true things I felt. We'd smile close, soft.

Then we'd disassemble. Baby back into her clothes, and me, washing and wrapping myself in a white bandanna from home. I'd uncork her favorite, Sancerre, and pour it into the gallery's murky wineglasses. I'd deliver it and light her cig as she stood before a half-hung, unstretched canvas.

One drunk time I said, I wish I could cum inside you.

You do, Baby said unthinking.

No, I mean, I wanna, I wanna really do it, I mean, I wanna get you pregnant. I wanna make a life out of our love. As I spoke, I ached with regret. It was the cringiest thing I'd ever said in my life. I felt hot red with shame.

Baby didn't say anything. Fuck. She walked to the canvas and started adding orange shapes with an oil bar. Come hold this up for me? she asked.

Paralyzed by my confession but holding the corner of the canvas up for her, I said, I'm sorry, I didn't mean— Baby cut me off. Not looking up from the canvas, she said, Yeah, I want that too.

It was still daytime. Evening's cool reprieve hadn't yet settled over me. Baby and Sophia sat at a café terrace in Oberkampf. As I approached, I heard Baby say, She's here. The "she," I knew, was meant to mean me. Beautiful with hurt, I sat down.

The plastic green-black-cream woven chairs, the red round tables rimmed in gold and cigarettes, the unbothered gazing, Perrier glistening on ice with a long spoon and a lemon slice, café allongé, pints, wine, restrained laughs and servers weaving through everyone's desire are a clutter I can usually relax into, that I can become. But it riled every tired scrap of me.

Baby kissed my neck to say hello. She wore a huge black T-shirt with a tiny, messily embroidered blue heart at her center. She was beamy and her warmth insisted that light reaches any depth. Sophia, as usual, was dead cool, with a shaved head, chunky ruby earrings and handsome, set laugh lines. Love your bomber, I said, lightly gesturing to the shiny, emerald silk sleeves that looked like paused water. Sophia said, Thank you. Baby said, Yeah, I've been wanting to get her the same one, and motioned to me. I drably noted their palpable sexual connection and touched Baby's leg under the table as if my hand alone would show her the truth of me. Baby shook her head and said the same sentence again with "him."

Can I ask about your gender? I was already sinking before I could answer. Sophia's directness felt so childlike, it almost made me laugh. Sure, I said. What about it? It's about being trans, she began. I mean, I'm sure you're aware of all these butch women becoming men. Don't you think we need to make a separate definition of butch?

I don't know. I shrugged, seeing she was serious, taking a sip of Baby's wine. I decided to ignore the surface of polite engagement and the sad prison Sophia's mind kept me in. I charged straight into the philosophical dimensions of her "question." I hinged my tone on the cusp of patronizing blankness: Does it feel like something is being taken from you?

No, Sophia said, no, but you, for example, you are moving away from butch into, well, manhood. I think being butch is a gorgeous, expansive thing, I told her. Who would a separate definition be for anyway? Some people are trans and some people transition and that's not your loss, I thought. That's not anyone's loss. I don't know what new definition is required, I said. You're talking about yourself as if you are everyone, Baby said, with her hand firm on my leg.

I leaned back, smoking. I met Sophia's mind again and tried nervously: I don't think masculinity belongs to anyone, like, there isn't one right way to do it. Sophia looked at me blankly, then furrowed as if in thought. I couldn't understand why my boyness warranted material for discussion. Sophia needed, somehow, to consult me on her separatist definitions. There's not one way to be masculine, sure, Sophia agreed.

But becoming a man, that's a crossing over. I looked at Baby, who looked at Sophia. I knew then that I didn't get to be one of them anymore. I was, in becoming true, antithetical to their likeness. I·leaned forward and put out my cigarette.

We ordered more wine and Sophia ordered a planche. She told us about her wife and kids and asked if we would ever consider kids. The question hovered in the air. I got the uneasy, familiar feeling that Baby wanted me to do something I couldn't. Sophia said Baby would be a great mother. Excuse me for a moment, I said.

I stood up and went to the bathroom. The hot, bright inside of the restaurant matched my mind's heat and was a truer environment. I spiraled down the stairs. The line for the door with a person in a dress was three-deep. I slid past and went through the door with a person without a dress. I locked the door and pulled the tiny baggie from my left front pocket. I looked at myself in the oval mirror. My skin was worn, an odyssey in my eyes. My core emptiness reached everything. My ability to be was in my heartbeat, heated with blow, helping me settle, letting me think. I need more already. I'll have to pick up again.

As I finished the lines and poured more of the baggie on my phone screen, there were knocks on the door that hustled me to finish. Too much spilled out of the bag and I sucked it up, checking my nose before leaving. I exited. The guy waiting looked me up and down and seemed mad. I ignored him as everything inside me radiated in fear.

C'est pour les hommes, mademoiselle. I walked past but he grabbed my arm and pointed to the door with a person in a dress. I jerked out of his grip as he called me something I chose not to hear.

Sophia and Baby looked good together, shoulder to shoulder. I felt dented. I couldn't speak. Words were only letters and letters were only lines made into silent shapes. I managed a smile and told them I had to run, chugging the last of Baby's wine. I kissed Baby and told Sophia it'd been a pleasure. Feeling like a guest in my own life, I made my way down rue Oberkampf, untethered from earth.

Toni, Paris

Toni's right. You're right, I say. We exit the métro stair by
stair. We're blasted by wind, soaked in evening. You can't fail
out of college, they insist. I know, I know, I say, lighting their
cigarette and then mine. We walk down rue Saint-Martin
and finish our smoke outside a queer bar, La Mutinerie.
You're almost done with it anyway, they say, glancing inside,
just do it. I knew I could finish my degree, but shapes larger
than institutions, than knowledge, than thought were taking over. I wish I was studying philosophy, they said. Yeah,
neuroscience must be hard, I said. I don't get how the brain
lights up in different colors. It seems fake, like a weather
forecast. Toni laughed and patiently told me something about
brain scans, then something about a dream.

Inside, the dance floor was sweating, compressed and
lurid. The bad speaker system played a bad mix by a DJ in
nipple tassels. I left Toni to the revelry and waded to the
bar. I always thought I could work at a bar, that the schedule would work for me. I'd like to be near the warm supply of
alcohol, shining behind me. I'd deal with all the stupid drunk

people in the dark with care, giving them more of what was already pulsing through me. I wouldn't stash drinks or hide. I'd just have to keep it together enough to stay standing, making drinks.

With a cold pint in my hand, I turned to face the dance floor again. On the right, windows were covered in posters. There were wobbly tables and packs of bodies. A royal blue light roiled over everything. I nodded at a person I knew from somewhere I forgot. Toni danced to the Styrofoam music with a shirtless boy. I pulsed in a brief electric calm, an almost safety, where my me-ness was a shrug or a long drag of a cigarette, a hot conversation out front, a laugh, a nod. Where I could exist at full volume, where the fact of me wasn't a disruption but an unquestioned, integrated fact of my being.

American Midwest

We listen to Antony and the Johnsons and stare frontward at
the dead football field. Tangles of bare tree branches frame a
yellow goal post. The gray morning light soothes. I hold coffee, a warm truth I chose to carry. Toni, going over their date
last week, tells me they want to be pursued. I tell them I want
to pursue. The song gets to be too much, and Toni gets out of
the car. I follow and stand with them on the hill before the
football field. This is where I dreamt I kissed our French professor last week, I tell Toni. Weird, they say.

They tell me they want to wear my uniform skirt. I laugh
at them for too long. They're serious. They're tall. Their dark
hair is gelled. I unroll and unzip my skirt. They unbuckle and
step out of their trousers. I look at the building behind me.
See no one. I slip into theirs, and they slip into mine.

Toni steps down the hill. My/their skirt, unzipped on their
hips, falls thoughtfully. They reach to hold on to it, pleats in
the wind. Their bare legs uninstall gender. I begin to feel a
blink of comfort, some software I don't have to update.

Using ink to make wings, I pull out my notebook. I lie wide, liking the long crotch of their/my trousers. With my weight leaning into my elbow on the hill, I watch a flock of birds go where we can't.

o

I'm writing a poem about my birth. Mom tells me about it. She tells me how her/my umbilical cord was wrapped around my neck three times. Funny, how I've always done things my own way. I've been unable to wane to some tide she named productive, suitable. Mom tells me this in between gulps of Miller Lite and inhales of menthol cigarettes. She tells me how scared she was, how she knew I was one of those babies born to run, so ready to leave her womb that I somersaulted right into an almost death. After lathering her with that orange numbing cream and sticking a syringe as long as a forearm into her spine, they cut her right open with a thick scalpel.

Dad was right next to her. His lips nearly touching her left ear. He sang Van Morrison's "Into the Mystic" in a low whisper.

I don't believe this but it seems like an honest attempt at sentimentality from Mom, so I'll keep it. That swimming-pool-blue sheet all she could see. It fell at her chest. She says it felt like a long time, and she grew more and more nervous that I was dying by my own accord, by her/my own noose. Her eyes go narrow as she tells me about the way her hips, legs and stomach were lifted from the surgical table three times as they tried to get me out. She says forceps eventually worked best. She touches the subtle dents on either side of my skull tenderly.

Dad says I was all blue and sickly when he cut her/my noose. Mom says I was pink, pink, pink and round and crying. Mom has never shown me her scar. She talks about the postpartum depression, though. She shows me a photo of her: rail-thin and in a white linen dress, her eyes empty and far, far off somewhere. My sister leans on her shoulder. I'm in her arms. She tells me proudly: Thinnest I've ever been.

I've grown to know that far-off stare. I walk into Mom's closet. I touch the waves of clothes, organized by season and color. Photos of Marilyn Monroe are posted on the wall by her vanity. She tries to keep her dress from exposing leg, thigh and ass. She's putting on makeup. She's posing for a photo. One gloved finger hangs from her open mouth. Her eyes have that same far-off gaze. She's somewhere else entirely. But her makeup, her dress, her smile, the photos, they keep her body present, propped up into the next play. It must be hard, being this beautiful.

Mom always wanted me to want to be beautiful. My bare feet hitting concrete, I was the fastest runner in the neighborhood.

Let me show you how far I've come. Once, in high school, I dared Dad to see what it is that makes me girl. This neighborhood. Dad and I were going for a run, right here. Saturday morning. A hot one. I took off my T-shirt. My heart, kicking under a gray sports bra. Wind graced my stomach, shoulders and arms as I tried to steady my breath, I could feel the wings of me unfold. He told me to put my shirt back on. I felt like he hated me. I hated this me too. I spit mucus on the hot sidewalk and let him run ahead. With my furnace eyes, I yelled: You wanted to be a chef but the condom broke, now I'm here.

Toni, Paris

On my cracked phone screen, I message long blocks of texts to Baby at the café table, with Toni next to me. They ordered us coffee. I leaned back into missing Baby:

Gravity obeys you, angel. Drink an ale or seven and fuck me rough. Besides punishment, what is it to be without your gaze, strong fingers and tongue for two weeks? Willing to do anything ever to you today. Any desire you voice, I obey. Back arched aching in solar want. My teeth pull on the meat of an olive. Gnawing at memories. I cum inside you.

Cloistered temporality / it's dense right here, the walls know / I miss all our sex materials / I'm thrown into a past moment of touch/ or / whatever

What lust structures can we fuck by? You know I like to breathe in the hurt skin between burn grip slap and hold. I want to live in the slice before I cum. With you, I live in these sought glistens of touch where I teach the matter of me that gravity makes spheres. I pull your fist inside me.

Baby how's it going? What shape is today? I love you.

Toni reads a page of last night's writing:

Q: *what is being trans other that undoing epistemology and*
     reapplying it to new parts and new feelings?

Q: *how could anyone understand the throes of gender and*
     not want to toss it off. Burn it. To disassociate from the
     assignment. All my philo profs gesture at this thing called
     choice. What fucking choice do any of us have? The way
     cells form in utero become imperatives for living. Everyone
     can fuck off with the whole two sides of a coin, binary shit.

A: *so, really though, are you a boy or a girl?*

A: *if our minds can construct a fiction like absolute time in*
     the universe manifest as small hands ticking, then we must
     build structures which are far less definite. One of these
     structures is the polarity of gender. Its scaffolding of hor-
     mones, body parts, gestures and clothes seems to support
     two entire, separate universes. The whole of gender is this:
     subjects socialized to behave, to identify, to believe in an
     ontological separation based on anatomy. But look, like
     time, it doesn't hold in all frames of reference. Gender is
     an ambition. It's a human fallacy, really. To white knuckle
     one measurement, building two antithetical ways of being
     when there are multi-fold, simultaneous dimensions of
     being within gender, within time.

Q: *but what's your novel actually about though?*

Toni and I take to the evening like it's our job. I don't have bookshelves in my room. I just stack. Toni knocked over a tower of them trying to find the hundred-euro bill we stashed for emergencies. It's in *Being and Nothingness*, I yell from the bathtub. No, no, it's in fucking Adorno, Toni yells. The guy is waiting. Toni throws on some of my dirty clothes from the couch and leans into the steamy bathroom. You're going to make the whole place even more of a sauna, they scold. I splash warm lavender water in their direction. Toni slams the door to get more blow. I submerge with each index clogging my ears.

They slam back into my apartment. I'm drying off. We're going to La Mutinerie, they demand.

I tie my towel at my waist and leave the heat of the bathroom for the heat of the living room. I stand and meet their gaze. It's different for a second, a light dims between us. They have a sleepless look, gorgeous brows. Their long dark hair is wild and sweat dews their face. Suddenly I want to feel them below me. On the bed, they hold the baggies up, crossing their left leg over the right. Their eyes seem to invite the largeness of my touch.

I sit next to them, taking the baggies. I kiss their wrist. I hear their breath and try to sync our inhales. We kiss slow and long. You taste like campfire, they say. Knowing my version of time and space was fundamentally ruptured, they slide my index and middle into their mouth. They meet my gaze.

Baby, I think. But Toni, I feel. They nod and I orient into their charged immediacy. Years of us meet, here, in this bed. My/their short black leather skirt shows more of them as they lie below me.

I shoulder into a binder, throw on a T-shirt and dip into one of the baggies. Toni lets the pink satin straps of their top fall off their shoulders. Their collarbones are irrevocable. Their gaze up at me ushers some wide angle of myself forward. They say no to the baggie, so I take more and tell myself they don't notice my habit, and if they do, they don't care.

I navigate kisses on their shoulders, neck and mouth. With the hard of me in their hand, I ask, What's your favorite way to cum? Like this, they said, turning over and bending before me. I take in the fundamental awe of their back. With one hand knuckled and tight on their smolders of hair, I make space for myself inside them. Dismal aches of day-to-day fall into generous obscurity.

After, they lie on my chest, smoking. I look at them and feel a tilt lighter, a tilt freer. I've never fucked like that, I say. Like what? Their tone holds the humor of our history. Like *that*. Toni nods. You mean like yourself. I look at the ceiling. I feel them try to find my eyes, and I say, Stop. Their assured sight wrecks me. They can see what I won't allow. They say softly, You're not used to people meeting your gaze? I close my eyes and nod. I know, they say, weaving an arm below me to hold me, I know.

Before I can escape sensation, thick, generous tears begin to fall. Toni faces me, propped up on their elbow. I know, they say again, I know, wiping my tears. I feel them watch me grab the baggie—my obsessional force wearing me, conducting me, becoming me. Toni kisses my forehead, smirks and opens the window wider, letting more of us out.

Kathy Acker, Every Tense

Kathy Acker: I like your posture.

Me: No, you don't.

Acker: Yeah, I do.

Me: I do not have posture because I do not have a body.

Acker: Shut up. You're arriving inside your body now, I can see it. Each night a little more of you gets inside and your posture tilts with.

Me: I want to look like you do in those black-and-white photos, the ones where you look all butch on a motorcycle—what did it feel like?

Acker: What?

Me: Having a body

Acker: It was hell until it wasn't anymore

Me: I think I want that hell.

Acker: The only thing you can't change is death.

Me: There will be scars on my chest. Are you repulsed by me?

Acker: No.

Me: I want to make love to you, with you.

Acker: We won't be making love. Fucking, maybe, but not
     love.

Me: Semantics. Can we put your words all around us in the
     bedding? Can you have a journal between your forearms,
     bent before me while I go deep inside, and the words will
     breathe out onto the page till you forget the pen till you
     forget you have a name—

Acker: You talk like you want to fuck the sun.

Me: Not the moon?

Acker: You walk like you could fuck the moon.

Me: I'm glad you came.

Acker: I think ghostdom suits me. How can you see all of me,
     even when I'm totally leaving myself and this body?

Me: I think I know God. I've come close enough. I had to kill
     parts of myself every day to be girl.

Acker: God is nothing but transcendence of body, maybe sex
     is an act of God.

Me: See, you fuck to leave your body, I fuck to get into mine.

American Midwest

And here I am again. I'm eight and with her—my best friend.
The willow tree hides us from the adults. The place she
makes me in. You be the boy, she demands. My heart snaps
around my whole body. Now, between my legs. Wind allows
tentacles from the willow to graze my banged-up knees.
The whole moment smells like woodsmoke. The mechani-
cal squish of trampoline springs in the distance. Who was
bouncing? Her small hands move mine from her shoulders to
her hips. Now, Romeo, now! I move into her warmth and kiss
her mouth. Her tongue goes in and out of mine. It was okay to
love it then. We were just playing.

When I was boy I knew what I would be. Just something big. Something where you stand tall and smile and think and run and sweat. But then the world got smaller. Details got bigger. Hems and eyelashes and shoes. What happened was they all said I was girl. I tried to believe them.

Toni, Paris

It's almost evening at our bar. It's Toni's last night. Shallow, maybe number 28, on rue Saint-Denis. Fifth or sixth beer on our shoes and on our lips that neither of us remembers ordering. Toni, next to me, maps the magnitude of desire. Little smog and hot breeze trickles the pages of their unlined notebook. After fervent discussion, we settle on a formula: $d = x^x$. Desire multiples itself, exponentially smirking. We knock at our fatal realization. I try not to consider their eyes too much. I look to the mess of this street. Baby and I live five minutes that way. Toni breathes, drinks and thinks one touch away from me. The smoking nexus of my own desire has a geography. This bar, this night.

The rolls of neon fabric bob, labored on shifting shoulders and the trotting, smoking mass on cobblestones. The syrupy swell of that boulangerie now masked by the tall thin man hosing down the poissonnerie across the street. Then my avoidance of Toni's eyes. Then the absent swallow. Toni goes on, my chosen cartographer. They write: *boy with wings.* Then they circle it and draw arrows spilling from the circle's edge. They stop, chew the end of their pen. I touch their leg under the table. I don't want Baby to be upset with you, they say. I know, I tell them, I know.

I finish my last inches of beer in one swallow. I ask the waiter for two more and tell Toni to follow me. They do, leaving their notebook open to the city.

In the bathroom, Toni chucks their too-full Jansport backpack on the sink and faces me. They run their touch from my neck to the crux of me. They whisper, Ponyboy. They go on touching the boy of me as I cut us lines. I'm not seeing myself from above, living lifted from flesh and feeling. No. With Toni's touch, I can be inside myself. I know by the way I shove them against the cold bathroom tile wall and bite down into the warm sky of their neck that they don't read me, they don't fuck me, they don't experience me as woman. Toni and I go on, navigating the surfaces of our queer flesh. Naming for ourselves, our selves. Toni's core is ocean. My cock is a swelling mast. We fuck with bruising grip, becoming true.

Later, we're back at the table, drinking deep. I'm rosy and damp and, despite the healing sexual landscape of Toni, I feel a tugging pull of guilt. I tuck away the thought that I want Baby to find us here. I deflate the rolling notion that I want her to see me fuck Toni and to leave me. Toni goes, You're so handsome post-cum.

We order more beers. Toni gives me half of a yellow square. I look closer, it's Pikachu. It's ecstasy. I don't want it, they say flatly. They look back at their notebook. I bite off half. It's dissolving chalk, suspended in my beer swallows. My index and middle shove the other half in my unusually deep pockets. I look at them and then at our formula, our magnitude. It appears like a museum caption below my frame of them—perfect. Then a little desire exponent hovers over their smirk.

Baby doesn't see me like you do. I know, Toni says, drinking their beer. I worried that when Toni left Paris, I'd stop existing to myself. Have her call you Ponyboy, they smiled, it suits you. You're a place to me, Toni. Well then walk through the door of me, they say. We both smirked at the gaudy truth of our connective affinity, love.

We get up and head out, leaving our beers to sweat and flatten in the quiet lull of our bar.

At gare du Nord, I'm only slightly rolling. I walk them to their platform. Travel safe—I hug them long and with a jealous grip. Before returning to Providence, they were off to see a man they knew in Nantes. He's a violinist, they said.

When I open the door, Baby's suitcase is open on the floor. She's hanging up a gauzy white button-down. You're back. I kiss her, quieting the panic that screams inside me. You smell awful, she says. I must reek of cum and beer and cigarettes. I put on the new album by No Thanks and change into a clean shirt.

Where were you? Baby asks, not looking up from unpacking. I was with Toni, at our bar. I immediately resent my announcement of "our." They've gone to Nantes. Baby asks, Nantes? Yeah, Nantes, I yell from the bathroom. Something about a violin and a guy. You made a mess of the apartment, she says, walking past the coffee table: the mirror laid for lines, empty green glass bottles, ash, loose change, empty orange American pill bottles, dirt from a spilled snake plant, a tiny plastic box spilling glitter, dried roses, a pocketknife and slices of printer paper covered front and back with fast ink.

As I start to clean it up, Baby says, Wait. She pulls out her phone and takes an aerial photo, smiling. I left it there, just like that, for you to get a photo, I joke. The colors are good, she says, motioning for me to sit with her on the couch. I grab two beers from the fridge and join. How was Sophia? I ask. What did you make?

I have a present for you, I say. I walk my middle and index down my pockets. I grin stupidly at the satisfying space of menswear. With a little broken Pikachu chunk on my damp palm, I propose, Please eat this glowy trinket of dopamine.

The high leaks in heavy. The evening has set now and the ecstatic yellow of our pillows bleed into one blinding embrace. Baby smiles, or if she didn't, I felt one—the intrinsic familiarity of being humans, having lungs, eyes, hair to touch, breathing in a room together. Baby swallows hers. I stroke her legs. She swings open a large pad of thick paper and starts to sketch.

We touch on the floor, on top of Baby's new sketches. Our human shapes on top of Baby's shapes on top of paper. Her form before me is a cohesive warmth. With the high, I become aligned with an uncomplicated delight, tangled in a gorgeous ache. I'm on top of Baby now, my breath on the fascinating slope of her neck. Suddenly my binder is an obstacle for breath. I briefly consider taking it off and run my fingers through Baby's hair. Every movement drips in swells of crashed light.

The next morning, I wake with a message from Toni: have more^ifyouwant. I cry most of the day, pathetically depleted, convinced my life is ending. Baby holds me and assures me that everything is not ending today, but that it's okay because it all will eventually, sometime, somewhen. Wow, I didn't think I bruised you that much last night, Baby says, I'm sorry. Guilt nearly suffocating me, I laugh, seeing Toni's breathy face, their open mouth. It's okay, I say.

Later, I respond to Toni: if you want^youwantmore. I can't help but lean toward the converging truths that Toni and I create together, into every sexual stumble where I feel seen.

To: paul preciado

Cc:

Subject: hey, an unsendable departure

I wanna apply your testogel. On your inner left thigh. Or right shoulder blade. Quick, sexy slide like the chemical inhale of a line. Banks of it, snow. I rub my right thigh on your left, taking up the cool gel. For you: one line. For me: two.

To make this simple is what I dream. But everything around me heats in shame. Me, trapped girl. Me, so boy. Look, I wanna revel in found boyhood. I wanna make loud the parts they strangle.

Maybe we'd lean, petty criminals, in Passage Molière. Inhabiting public space. Defining our place in it. Firmly sliding into position, unafraid of death, of rape. To seize that sick luxury.

I wanna sit across from you a while. While you think. I'd look back then up like I do from your pages. With my knowing, sweaty smirk, I'd show you that this body is all I depart from.

I'd show you what you showed me: new slopes of this ancient sphere. |

Baby, Paris

This isn't a poem. It's my biggest fear:

*Chop off my chest / you're my surgeon just cut me open /
pull out the tissue and / feed it to your dog / he's a good boy
/ like me / adrift and afraid of the name they / gave me he
can't make this about my / social capital again / Baby cries
I say / it's murder the way no one is stunned / by your form
/ lit from behind / the loud cars get fucked by rain / later
/ her handsome, veiny hands hold up / Catherine Opie's
photos / this is it / she / shoves it in my face: / a woman with
a cartoon home cut into her back / this one is it for you / you
hold the knife at your own back / but instead of words I /
surrender to something ancient / churned-up desire melts
into another aimless
hand job engrossed in / sticky affection cumming / again
and again Baby says / we're fucked / and at dinner I'm tying
Baby up / their conversation lulls and praises and then dies
/ drunk eyes glance over at me / me, perversely fingering the
thick metal ring / it's loud and I look unhinged but / men-*

tally I'm hooking it all together / Baby's tiny wrists here and her torso on the table / my cock / blank, raw / harder their table conversation goes on in that language I won't learn / I told you Baby I told you / I told you / you erode my solitude you golden / slut

American Midwest

Orange tiger lilies grew on the side of the house. Their mischievous glow coming right at me. Little spots of dew, I want
to remember, and the pulpy brown residue at the tips of their
antennae. Sexy. My mind inserting memory. I rub the brown
powder between my fingers.

The side of the house was a place to be alone. The backyard,
with its play set and shallow hill, was easily seen through
the kitchen window. The front yard, with the monkey swing,
was good too but felt too easily observable—neighbors, cars,
people walking by. I learned the front was not a place to play
that time Mom took away blankie. You're too old to carry it
around, it's dirty, it's time for it to go. Where is blankie gonna
go? Somewhere better, Mom said, and nodded, crouching to
meet my watery eyes.

I went to the front yard. I approached the curved turquoise
plastic of the swing. I looked up at the tunnel of yellow rope
that Dad chucked onto the oak's thickest arm. I followed the
yellow back down. The swing fell at my nose. I stood like

a fucking saint: loved Mother Mary and her strong eyes. I chucked the swing away from me with both hands and closed my eyes and clenched for impact. My aim, exact. It took six smacks before I felt that warm drip on my mouth and then my tongue. Tastes like rocks, I remember thinking. The same chemical drip I now savor after several fat lines. One. Two. Three. Four? Four. Ah. Tastes like rocks.

Even as the blood came down I knocked myself again with the swing, for good measure. I kept my eyes open that time. The momentous pendulum of the swing felt like a sea-green moon, flung in and out of its orbit around an invisible planet that loved me and blankie. I went up the cement steps, past the porch, and into the house. Mom, I cried immediately, I'm hurt! Oh, honey, your shirt, she lamented. I need blankie! And I got what I wanted. Mom handed me the tattered white cotton of my love and cleaned up my bloody nose.

After that it was ruined. Mom wanted to have someone watch me play when I was out front. The side yard, I decided. The tiger lilies my only witnesses. I had brand-new red gloves on. I want to remember that I was reading to the lilies but that's probably not true. Maybe the book about dolphins was closed on the grass next to me. I conducted like Dad showed me in the opera video. My bunch of fiery friends and my red hands bounced, pushed, pulled, caressed.

I let out one of my hourly operatic belts. I secretly decided my life as an opera singer would only work if I was also, simultaneously, the conductor. My private singing performances were a surefire way to give away my location.

———

After an acutely vocally exhausting part of my show, I fell
to my knees to catch my breath. I chivalrously took off a red
glove and offered it to the blank form of air to my right. I don't
remember seeing anything there, I just looked at the distance
with a reverent gaze. When I returned from my romantic
gesture, my sister was there. Her sandy blond hair, smile and
massive green eyes. Time for dinner, she offered. That was
enough for me. With my ungloved hand, I punched her right
in the nose. Doesn't it taste like rocks?

Dora, Every Tense

Dora,

Your case. Freud's psychoanalysis of a young hysteric. Dora. Your father's friend tried to kiss you when you were fourteen. His erection, pressed on your pelvis. Freud can't understand why a girl would be revolted by such advances. Freud says your unconscious repression of his erection manifested in a sore throat.

And then there's the lake. Dora would sit there and smoke cigarettes. Her father's friend followed her there—her place to be alone. He followed and rolled her a cigarette. She took it. She was low on tobacco. And he pressed himself onto her, into her. She slapped him and ran from her fortress by the lake. She ran out of the only room she had. She took a nap on her bed. There was a soft evening glow and the smell of her father's tobacco. She opened her eyes and there he was again. Standing over her. She asked her father for a key. To lock her door. To keep him out. He refused.

So she stopped sleeping. Developed a cough, chronic. Severe appendicitis. Focused pain throughout the lectures she attended. In her books. In her dreams and waking life. Freud said this pain was a pregnant fantasy since it lasted for nine months after the lake incident. Freud said she wanted her father's friend to impregnate her. Freud said any girl attending so many lectures, reading so many books, must not be trusted to have the customary sexual desire for men. Freud said that masturbation led her to a deviant desire for women—her announcement that the governess's body was: adorable, white.

Freud was analyzing his own conscience. His own repressions. The consciousness of his time. Not Dora's. Dora, do you want to hang out?

I have a room of my own. We can share it. We can go to lectures. There are queer people on the street. They drive past this man vs. woman thing, see it's all cracking open. Smirks and turns and thousands of palms to the imperatives of gender. Dora, they're churning in something ancient. Turning over that heavy stone. We're still here, Dora.

We can detract our energy from the colossal categorical. Look, we can put it back in our muscles and our minds and our laughter. We can go to the lake if you want. We can sit shoulder to shoulder. I'm not so good at rolling cigarettes, so you'll have to manage that. You can kiss me. Dora. Hysteria isn't a diagnosis anymore. It's just an insult men call women and other women call women. Dora. Do you want to have dinner? I'll make you ratatouille and lemon cake. Did you write poems? Can you read me some? Your history hasn't been told and I need to know. I need your words. I'm begging for your story.

I wonder where you are, Dora. I listen for your songs, for your breath. I linger here. I walk over there. I lie on my bed in my own room. I have a key, Dora. Do you want to come over? Do you want to dance, to drink some wine? Your hands smell like lavender and ash, I know. There's orange paint under your fingernails, I know. There's a manifesto in your head and it's moving with your every step, I can tell. Maybe we can see a show, I'll buy you pints.

I know you can't come. I know you're gone. Dora, I know, we know.

But I want to know your furrowed brow. Freud says you stood before Raphael's *Sistine Madonna* for two hours in dreamy admiration. That's exactly how I find myself in front of you.

You didn't say why you stayed so long.

You just said: Madonna. Madonna. Madonna.

Dora. Dora. Dora.

Baby, Paris

Baby is on her back. The light is gray. In a poppy-red hoodie, she wears the tight, thick black jeans that are sewn in her genius.

She's got her arms splayed out on the electric-green of a shallow hill, just before it meets the piss-soaked shrubbery of Jardin des Tuileries. I greet her, touching the poem folded in my left pocket. I hug her long, as if to say, I'll always protect you. My loving, inked hand on her lower back, we walk.

Baby steps ahead, in front of me, gesturing to the statues scattered on the green. Usually we come here for an inexpensive night of getting fucked up. Bottles of wine in this country are cheap, cork tugged and drunk straight from the green glass. This part of the jardin doesn't close. It's also central enough that everyone can at least stop by on their way somewhere else. The Louvre and its shady authority loom in view.

In the dim afternoon light, there are children tottering around, a truck sells bad croissants and white gravel dust exhales up and around the Arc de Triomphe du Carrousel. A

O

man sells things that light up, things that fly. Another sells beer. I buy one for Baby, two for me. We keep walking.

A cold gust, love, brims over me. I look for her eyes and meet them. We've stopped under the right, smaller arch in the arc. From the corner, a man plays something slow on a violin. Its warmth coats us. I lean back on the limestone wall behind me. I light Baby's cig and savor this spill of sensation, this stupefying affection. We stay there, smoking and drinking at each other.

I didn't want her to know how precious this all was to me. I didn't want her to see how full she made me. With her, entire conceptual lives unbound and became real. My eyes, with Baby, were allowed the romantic burden of tears. I wiped one away before taking her in the crux of my arm and walking forward. Baby opened my second beer with her lighter, saying: If we want to get in, we must go down.

Sophia let her skip an entire day of studio work. The only requirement was that she had to go to the Louvre and look at the *Muses Sarcophagus*. She was also told to bring me along, which seemed like a power move. The Louvre is all empire: stolen artifacts, stolen histories, genocides silenced in the walls of this glossed-cold, slick palace.

We crossed rue de Rivoli and dipped underground at Palais Royale–Musée du Louvre. We took the white-tiled path up past the platform. Dark blue signs with arrows told us where to go. Baby, always a little ahead of me, looked back just as I took a short swallow from the cold flask in my coat. I caught up and we took the hallway up to the busy mall under the glass pyramid, through security and the bulky line and then, finally, to the Denon Wing.

This just doesn't inspire me, Baby says. We look down at the Roman casket, the muses in stone cloth look about: comedy, dance, poetry, music. When I die, put me in this glorified, lidded bathtub. Baby doesn't laugh but scans the perimeter. Sarcophagi are cool in that they represent the anxiety of death, she says to the ceiling. If I can control the vessel my dead body lies in, I can control death. The ancient-est of anxiety, I agree.

Do you see yourself in this? What? This—she points to the sarcophagus. I let myself go, knowing Baby protects my thinking by challenging it, by considering, by asking. Well, I begin, I like the idea of a muse musing, being the object and the inspired at the same time. Your own living, the generative force. Like the muse isn't this outside angel, brisk with inspiration, dipping in and out of your life. To wait for inspiration is to wait for death: like how this sarcophagus operates, exactly. The muses are in stone in a wishful circumference around the dead. I think the act of living itself is more than enough to keep me making. I don't wait for a tangential deity to strike me into meaning, into creating. My breath does that.

Baby follows my track, then there's these muses musing other muses—that's what we're doing, isn't it?

She has me by the hand, pulls me into her. I smile, knowing she's living without waiting too. I kiss her with history's nervous grip. We exist, despite the inevitable doom, our someday death. People wander past and watch. They all have phones instead of faces.

Baby wasn't even that upset when I told her about Toni. She just needed to take a walk alone. We had made our way through two bottles of whiskey and a bit of blow. I didn't even mean to say it, it just happened in a clumsy rush.

When she came back, she confessed she slept with Sophia several times over the summer. I looked at her and we just kind of sat there for a moment, a cool night air rustling the limp petals in the vase by the window. We agreed it would be stupid to break up about this, that love should set us free and whatever else.

Baby looked suspicious but sat beside me, passing the plate with a line for me. I told her about the sex, omitting the night at the bar. I tried to explain how being with Toni made me sure of who I am. I'm not a lesbian, I'm, kind of, well, I'm not a woman.

The silence was sharp. I knew the optics of Toni and I didn't suit her furiously gorgeous art-world landscape. Baby didn't know any other trans people. She didn't actively dislike them but also didn't make any effort to see them as viable, present and real.

She grabbed my hand. But it's not you, she said, *you're* not the same. I felt an electrical, evaporative heat. A passive hope fled me. Sitting next to her on our couch, I was a mere blankness. I'm sorry, I said, tucking myself away. Forget it, I assured her, it's not like that. I lit a fresh cigarette, the paper made blue in the dark. I looked at her as she cut more lines, nodding to some band I forgot I liked. I looked for her gaze as she passed me the plate. She needed to read something I just couldn't write. I took what she offered out of fear and put my hand on her leg. She climbed on top of me and as we touched, a base level of shame became me. Don't, I said, moving her hand from the hard of me.

Her eyes were soft, looking me over from above. She lowered and let her arms rest on my shoulders, her hands dangling behind my back, knees bent on either side of me. Sounds from the street below softened. Her hair was touched by the wind. How dare you, I'm still me, I thought as I moved my hands over her waist and hips. She leaned into me and offered: I want *you*, Ponyboy. Which me? I asked flatly. You, just you, she said in my ear. But I am me, I said. She kissed my neck.

I'm undoing her jeans, kissing my way down as I pull. I drag her to the edge of our bed and find myself slowly inside her. After my mouth, my hand. She goes to undo my trousers and I shake my head, smile and pin her to the bed by her wrists. Not tonight, I say, kissing her neck as I press deeper into her. Toni, I thought, Toni. I ached then, thinking Toni was a memory that may have just, after all, been a really good dream.

Every Tense

"I"

It's impossible to talk about you. Still, I try. What you can and can't be to me. The stories we knock at. I'm not sorry I haven't named you. You were named so many times, but none settled. You're the entry point. A threshold to pass, splash, dive in and out of. A place to conduct my tribe of ideas, this wobbly architecture. Us, arms open on the edge of ontology. I blow air into the balloon of you and let my living float off wherever you take me. I do like you. But I don't know too much of you that I don't know of myself. Look, here. Bite. Pull.

You're the swallow of this story we're untelling.

-I

negative two:
drunk localities

The cab took Baby and me away. We went up the boulevard de Magenta to gare du Nord. I teared up thinking about the books I couldn't bring. I left them stacked on the sidewalk, hoping for the best. Baby, kind about it, reminded me it was okay to let your library go. I saw Joel-Peter Witkin's photos open to the wind on someone's desk. I saw *Zipper Mouth* by Laurie Weeks on the stairs of the métro, pink and wanting to be held.

We left when I finished my degree in philosophy. Baby got a job as a curator at a big gallery in Berlin. Thankfully, I'll never have to use my political science degree, she joked. I hadn't been before but Baby assured me I'd like it. I knew of writing workshops there. She sounded alive and hopeful when she spoke about it, so I agreed.

We'd spent the night before with everyone, but when the sun started showing, we kicked them out. We cleaned and packed. I felt mobile, spontaneous and miserable. We didn't have more than several suitcases, tall, rolled canvases and two backpacks, urgent with books and filled journals. The roots of me went wide, not deep. Baby leaned her head on my shoulder. The cab trudged us to a stop. I watched her wings fold for the pause before our exit.

Hefting our material life from the trunk, we stood outside the chaos-station and smoked with our shared clutter.
Baby rested on my chest and I tried for stability. We made it
to the platform and watched the faded red train screech in.
No parting words to our home of five years came to mind.
Nearly everything then, except Baby, became a shrug. I felt
innocent, a martyr for being alive. Me, praying, arms up in
submission to the heavy desolation of my life.

I sadly accepted the dragging shape of forward motion. I
lifted the things of us onto the train with muscle-clenched
reverence while Baby found our seats. The train pulled forward and I walked wide in the opposite motion, back through
the corridor, and found Baby. All I wanted to know about
knowing came from this Paris. I saw Baby and I vanish from
each narrow street, canal perch, damp bar, café and park
hill. I took Baby's hand because touch alone could save us
from becoming memory. I slouched deep in my seat and saw
nothing but the heavy green out the window as we moved to
another city in another language.

The apartment was nice. It was ours. A bit dingy, yes, with corners too dusted to ever totally clean. Too small for all our living, yes, but there was a balcony where the sky was closer, a place for me to breathe. We loved on Zossener Straße.

Baby dragged the bed to the center of the room when we moved in. She bent me over the creaking headboard. We hung warm lights and stuck unframed photos and drawings on every wall. Baby laid out a tarp and set up a place to paint in one corner. My writing desk was shoved adjacent.

When we worked, we became a diagonal force, the space between us pushing me to page and her to canvas. It was mutual that way. We'd take breaks and smoke. Baby would read me poems she'd written in her head. One called "these walls are not walls" never left me. She'd hand me a black oil pastel and let me write out a line or two wherever I chose on her current painting. I'd breach her still, simple colorscapes with my scrappy, jagged lines. Somehow, she made violet look like wind, yellow as deep and crumbly as pollen.

Once, Baby did a performance piece where she sang a Brazilian gospel song, barefoot in a tiny bikini. With a flogger and microphone in hand, she strutted across the crowded gallery, flogging herself red.

I continued making at my own pace across from her. Poems made the most sense then, and I'd write several a day in between fits of research. She trusted what I saw in her work. She liked my writing enough to be honest and made my words feel truer to myself. We found ourselves in a city wide for making with huge sidewalks and high ceilings. DIY galleries, small gigs, readings and long parties every night. It seemed everyone we came across was doing some kind of creating too. Apart from the stark architectural weight and bland food, it felt cerebral, wild and luxurious compared to Paris.

Baby needs it clean, the whole place. The beige bathroom tile. Messy is fine, not dirty. I like the bleach smell best. I take the fresh laundry drying on the balcony inside. I clean the mirrors, sweep the loud wood floors. I devotionally leave the dripped wax on the tables and floor. I never touch Baby's paints or canvases. I never cleaned much before. Baby told me to grow up about it and so I did. Blow helped too. I'd bend my hangover into a speedy cleaning fury and feel accomplished enough to start drinking again.

Mouthwatering, I'd open the first beer of the rest of my life and sit at my desk to look for work. The blue Craigslist links always seemed to suggest I keep pretending I'm a woman and fuck for money. I wasn't brave enough for that. Instead, I'd look for nanny gigs or vaguely creative jobs before writing a bad poem or two and drinking through all we had. I'd watch old live recordings on YouTube. I was transfixed with one of the Cramps playing "The Way I Walk" at a psychiatric hospital in '78. I cried. Lux Interior, looking alive, starts the song saying, "We drove three thousand miles to play for you people. Somebody told me that you people are crazy. I'm not so sure about that. You seem to be all right with me." The fuzzy recording made me want to be a body scream-singing to people like me.

I'd be alone, mostly, not knowing who to be around or where friends could be. Baby worked late. She'd come home or wouldn't or would text me the address of a party or show. I'd need more to drink. The späti below made me ache. It was fluorescent in an American way. Berliners then felt so cold and old, rude and grunting. I'd get all that I could hold, hoping to have enough left on my card. The monthly funds from Dad were generous but wore thin quickly. He'd continue to send me money as long as I was doing a workshop or trying to find a job. His support gave me a closed-off kind of focus, a spacious pressure to succeed.

Sometimes I'd just keep the drugs and alcohol to myself and stay in drinking and listening to music and writing in brief exhales. Sometimes I'd meet up with Baby and whoever and talk to people and feel close to the night but never to myself. There were always so many things other people could talk about. I had a hard time looking up from the floor.

I called Toni last night, smoking on the balcony before going out. They told me I've lost my intellectual edge. I think they meant I've lost my mind. I told them to come see me. I imagined them signing up for the workshop with me, us walking in together, thinking wide. They declined, explaining with a patronizing sigh that they must stay in Providence to finish their degree.

They said I need help, that people like us don't survive addiction. But I'm not an addict, I said. I decided to never tell Toni about drugs again and calculated how much blow was left—I'd need to call the guy. Toni sounded small and hurt through the speaker of my hot phone screen, pressed to my cheek: You don't think you drink too much? Don't think you do too much coke? I furrowed with insult, rolling my eyes. Toni, what do you mean, people like us? Trans people, they said.

Baby listens. Or it seems as if she does. Constant revelry isn't revelry at all.

It's morning for us, which means it's another evening. We wake tangled in the ache of comedown. The hangout last night started as beers on the steps of that church in Schillerkiez. Then we chucked ourselves to Körnerpark. Blow and G and ketamine, alcohol, whatever. As the sun began to rise, Baby offered me acid, her eyes one massive black circle with webs of red on the glassy white rest. I laid my arms out, my back on the shallow hill slope as she laid the tab on my crucifix tongue. It was time to end and float into the gray sky.

No death yet, I thought, no. To prove I would not become the sky, I hinged my elbow on the hill and sat up. I took in the bodies around me. There were only five of us left. Baby's friends generally became my friends. She seemed to like the photographer in the blue hoodie a lot.

Everyone looked so fucked and brilliant. Rants were slurring. Someone peed in the bushes. Another person returned with a crate of beers, finally. Two others were nearly making love. I briefly imagined everyone's parents, seeing their queer outcomes sharpen into scary, daylight creatures. The hedonist, urgent eyes of everyone ate away at me. I crawled down the hill to the beers.

Toni, I thought. I need Toni.

I wake up between Baby and the photographer. He says he loves my tits, while snorting something I reckon is speed off a massive dinner plate. Baby rolls over to face him and me. Did we all fuck? I think we did. I look at my chest and nearly vomit at his dry crusted cum. I'm not your blank canvas, you unoriginal fuck. Give me the plate, I say, taking a line.

I sludge from bed, rub him off my chest and put my binder and T-shirt on in the bathroom. I make us all coffee while the photographer arms into his blue hoodie and loads his Pentax with a new roll of film. Baby hasn't painted lately. She focuses on curation and making chairs in the Hinterhof. I hardly use my desk, never really read. Since our first month here, I haven't made anything except poem notes in my phone. The workshop, my reason to not totally erase, starts in one week.

We use my desk for empty bottles. Many of my books remain unread, Baby and I rarely fuck. If we do, it's a dire, anarchic experience. I don't remember much of it, or anything, which feels right. Are you coming to the opening later? Baby croaks to each of us and neither of us. The photographer looks at Baby through his lens as she extends for him on the bed, a hot mug steams on the bedside table by her face, the plate of lines sits in front of her chest. His trigger clicks and a flash chaotically blooms in gray light. I blink to save a better version of his photo, slam the door to the balcony and stare far, far off somewhere.

Baby's installed mounds of powdered milk all over the floor that drunk people track around. The whole space becomes Baby's with her white powder beautifully everywhere. She makes moqueca in one massive pot on a hot plate, everyone watches. She gives strangers steamy bites with her grandmother's wooden spoon. When she approaches me, she kisses my neck and slides a bite into my mouth. I whisper in her ear: I love this.

You've left your mark, I cheers Baby and the photographer. Her orientation swooshes to him most of the night and I don't really mind. He has speed, so he's good company. We all go to the gallery bathroom after a smoke. The photographer and I each do a line off Baby's thigh. Then we all move to the back of the gallery.

There's a DJ set and everyone is sweating and moving. Their feet drag around Baby's snow. The photographer tries to kiss me as I kiss Baby. I keep moving, looking at the DJ, taking up space.

Before long, I'm over it. We go back to the bathroom. We all do lines. Baby turns to look at me and kisses me slow. The photographer is undoing his pants. He looks at Baby and me. Baby and I stop and look at him. He's hard and holding himself. He's handsome in a clumsy way. A tall guy, with soft eyes. He's always in primary blue, which seems intentionally calm. His proximity this way, though, makes him a menace, stirring me. He looks at us like he wants us to hurt. Moments of last night come back to me. I choose to forget.

Someone pounds at the door, the critic Baby loves is about to leave. She pulls up her jeans and limbers back into her leather blazer. She leaves with a smile and a slam.

The photographer just looks at me. He kisses my neck. I wince and bite back hard. You're so beautiful, he posits to no one, turning me around. He undoes my trousers, pulling them down over my ass. My body tightens as I push him off and stand to face him. I tell him to fuck off. He blinks at me, surprised. Leave, I say. He takes a second to adjust himself and leaves, annoyed. A person waiting for the bathroom with a cool mullet, lime-green bikini top and gray trousers tries to come in as he exits. He stops them and says something I can't hear as I shut and lock the door. I smile at the baggie he left on the sink and, finally, I'm alone.

The lavender glitter on my eyelids keeps me going. My hair is parted in the middle. It's dyed flat black. The skin below my eyes sags dark, as if slightly bruised. It looks like I haven't really slept in weeks because I haven't. Rest is faint, even in memory. I wear a white binder and white tank under Toni's white hoodie. I smell the neck for traces of them. I wear loose white jeans and white Air Force 1s. I am an icy, silent island. I stop looking at myself before I notice how unlike myself I look.

My mind flares back to the baggie. I bend from my reflection and pour it all on my phone, not bothering to cut lines. A numbed-out surge blasts me. My heart affirms every fear. Everything bad *is* happening inside me but my heart also declares every good trait I've ever resembled. I'm incredible. I'm attractive. I'm the cleverest light as I run my fingers through my hair in the mirror and finish my beer, looking at myself from my side glance—chest flat, check. I exit with quick grace, simply tough, angelic. The person waiting in green loves me. Glints of meltless snow are in my hair, on my lips. I float for another drink, taking in the brilliance of Baby's shining mind translated here in this gallery, for all these people.

The photographer finds me at the makeshift bar, which floats high like me. What the fuck do you want? I ask, towering over him. He says he wants me. I look for his eyes as I swallow curt, acidic pulls of bad wine from a plastic cup. Something deep and far away comes up and near. The music feels good now, like it's a part of my body. I feel his desire project onto me as my own. I nod at him. The dream of more drugs and keeping this height sparkles. In this exchange, anything is possible.

We both half check that Baby is occupied with people. She is. I float behind him, past the line at the bathroom and the dance floor. I look down and see the powdered milk tracks my sneakers make even as I float above. That's how smart Baby is, I briefly think. She keeps me on earth even when I'm this high.

He takes me to the back office. I didn't know he had the key. He wants me over the desk and says so. A line first, bitte. He gives me several and I magnetize all the powder up my nose to my brain. I think about lobotomies as he bends me where he wants me. I lift even higher, not feeling the desk or papers below. I do feel his depth, it's a sensation that spreads through every limb, like a tension that releases intravenously into nonhuman calm.

He's a fast, declarative fuck, a relief for the situation. He calls me something I choose not to hear as he goes harder. Where do you want me to— He cums on my low back. I remain focused, thinking this is funny, more white in my life. I use his blue hoodie to clean him off and get back into my white jeans. We do more blow and I face him, suspended. I kiss him soft until I feel the hard of him again. Still floating, I coax three grams off him.

As I turn to leave, he pulls me by my back pocket to face him. He puts his massive hands on my shoulders. We look at each other and I try to hide my fear, to tuck any of myself away. He moves down to the crux of me and I hate his touch. I ask for a line. I float again. He sits on the wobbly office chair, taking me with him. Knelt and holy, I take him throat-deep till he's done. I stand up and chase him with bad wine, looking down at his stupid calm spread in the chair. He drags me in by my waist, closer, slipping another gram into my left pocket.

Later, in the almost-empty gallery, Baby tells me the critic liked it. I smile wide. Congrats, Baby, congrats. Are you into him? She points at the photographer. No. Why? I say, sweating-nervous but still tall. I think I am, she says, not looking at me. Okay, I say, annoyed. But if you don't want me to, I won't. It's not that deep, I say, taking a drink.

I like that he has speed, I say, feeling good that I can at least tell that truth. Then someone else, taller than my tall, runs into me as Baby walks toward the photographer's older, vaguely cool group of friends. The photographer looks for my eyes and summons me over. His blue sweatshirt is tied around his waist. I look through him and glance back at my phone. Baby chats with someone whose haircut makes them look like a tadpole. I head out, feeling marked. Kissing Baby, my only goodbye.

At home I lie alone on our altar in my white tank top, my arms crossed behind my head. My whole body buzzes above me. I climb with thoughts, the crash coming my way. I think of Baby and that guy and plot a way to show her how awful he is, to get him out of our lives, but language is too fast a force to solidify.

Sensation, no, I'm cold blank, alone. I finish half of the speed and feel pure for not doing it all. I drink a bottle of whatever and try to sleep. I keep the windows open wide, the lull of club kids and bike gears making me sweat.

In the morning, I touch Baby's cheek and kiss her lightly. I run my finger over her thick eyebrows like she loves. Like the way Mom did to me. I see Mom reading Jane Austen to me in the tub. Her tan hands and long hair. I floated with the name Darcy, a name I could want. Mom closed her book and left for a second. She'd come back smelling like Chanel and tobacco, wrap me up out of the warm water and sink me into bed, where I'd dream.

What dreams do I live with ink on page /how do I know which words and when / how do I know I'm man / except that / I do, that / I am

Earnest, Baby told me the photographer makes art about relationships. I laughed back: Sounds conceptually *really* original.

We ate toast, cucumber and olives for breakfast at sunset on the balcony. She smiled and told me to shut up. Both grinning, we kissed awkwardly, sweetly. I winced at the memory of the photographer and me. Baby may understand, but the transactional harshness of it all felt too dark to communicate—the moment proved something dirtier in me, a gnawing impulse, unfeeling and insatiable.

We're at the same gallery as before, it's always the same fucking gallery. Baby's still everywhere: the white floors have traces of her powder. I approach Baby, smiling, and dodge a huge, inflated cock that the photographer hung from the ceiling. It's beige and veiny and makes me gag a little. The balls of the thing are massive gun-shaped balloons. Attached to the shaft are dozens of passports.

What do you think? the photographer asks. I look at him blankly and ask where his blue hoodie is. Baby touches my shoulder. As if it's my greatest fucking achievement, she explains that I don't act like I know what contemporary art means. Looking at the massive cock above my head, I ask, Anybody wanna line?

I get wrung on speed, wine and ketamine, totally flimsy but awake and chucked forward by my terrifying life. I wonder what is left of that guy's supply and if he'll tell Baby about the back office. I hate that he's in my thinking now. Baby and I smoke out front. I ask if she gets that guy's art.

I think it's a neoliberal power phallus, fucking us into an identity, she says. Smart, I say, so what identity do I fuck into you? I wait. She takes a drag. The street is quiet. The gallery's insides match my insides: warm in movement. You fuck me into a dyke. She laughs, kissing me. A distance settles. Baby, no, I'm not a lesbian. You know what I meant, she says.

Let's get out of here. She smears her cig out with her pink sneaker. I'm relieved to leave. Inside, we move through clusters of bodies. We wave goodbye to various overdressed people drinking wine. Then Baby hugs the photographer goodbye, and he smiles at me over her shoulder.

We exit together, her long, thin arm is stretched back to me, and I take her hand. I look back and watch the photographer watching us go. Baby, I say. Yeah? You're not even a dyke all the time and I'm not a dyke ever. Yeah, yeah, Baby says with a laugh, calm down with all that wine. This upsets me into needing another drink. I make Baby stop at the smoky bar on our road. Our table in the back is open. Dozens of long maroon candlesticks are the only light. She looks amused, across from me. We each do a shot and sink into our pints. She asks me, generously, What color is your novel today?

What else? The yellows, I guess. Maybe that heated orange in the Hinterhof. I steer right into it. My form still wants to fold over the chilly iron rail and fall with gravity. Baby goes, It's time, and she means another night of vodka mate. Yes, that yellow. Or the yellow slosh of clinking pints. Then, maybe some K on the canal or in a loud dark warehouse vibrating in repetitive blasts that I don't give a fuck about. In clubs, I crouch in a corner and look at people sweating out their vices or I dance for a minute. For now, I pivot on the balcony looking out at the nearly dead leaves, their expiration in wind and then sky and then ground. They coat cobblestone in one peeling autumn joy pasture.

I saw a performance last night at Madame Claude where a guy had a variety show. He had an orbit of beautiful young women dancing around him, checking his amp, passing him his guitar, getting him a drink, smiling. It made me suspicious and a little sad until a performer in a cream slip started throwing cold, damp leaves around from a gray plastic bag. I held a fistful and threw them at the man. I got him right in the guitar.

Tonight, the party is inside but I choose here. Here, on planet balcony. My strapped-on antenna grows hard in my

thick black jeans. The cock of me leads skyward, drunkward.
I pivot back and look at the oranges of inside: people I know,
people I don't, nodding to that Pavement album I demanded
from out here, then caving over a few lines. They resemble
children hunched over a new game, fingers desperate to peel
the plastic so they can divide up roles. The white powder in
our bloodstream, another hearth glowing.

I know what I want and maybe what I mean to say but
not how. That's the smear of my life here, the how of it all.
Going out with nowhere to be, really. But all of us using each
other as a place to exit. Each other, a place to have a stare-off
thought, each alone, in unison. Baby comes out to coax me
in, puts her head on my shoulder, whispers, Ready? But the
leaves are still going, I say.

Mostly, here, I'm dissimilating like one glacier chunk
beaten by sun. Foreign, again. One massive semantic crack
and I split and bob into a melted version of myself. Mostly,
here, I'm walking in opaque, unarmored confusion. This
city isn't a skinny smog, cigarette, shit river like Paris, it's
worse. It's darker in its expanse. Look—I wink at Baby—I can
walk with my arms out and touch no one. These streets and
sidewalks rest like I do. Like my legs do: wide but uninvit-
ing in bars, at readings. My knees are as wide as the Berlin
pavement, these isolating avenues I tread: Hermannstaße,
spreading and lonely. The canyon that explosive destruction,
rape, war, and genocide made. Recent history screams with
me and my wide steps in fear, in void. The empty of burnt
books. Yes, that yellow too.

I crawl drunk and desperate in the devastation of forty

thousand people looking onto a fire, sharp like tiger lilies one night in '33 at Opernplatz. Magnus Hirschfeld's research, trans history set alight. The books are not even memory. No, they are evaporated ash fluttering in air. My scorched history, I breathe it in with decadence, with deference, with the weight of my identity held in dead lovers' hands. We walk forward into night. Into my shapeless life of queer duck-and-cover.

Baby's arm is wrapped around my shoulders and her wrist bobs and guides us. I'm fish, baited by her from below. I follow along like that. Someone dances ahead. Baby nods with the drugs. The dull acoustic of this city is made electric with the leaves. We stop under a sloped orange neon sign. Baby ask the photographer if we should all fuck tonight. Someone howls at the moon. I shrug along, my eyes far, far off somewhere. What else?

I find Baby reading in bed alone. Hey, my love. I crawl in next to her after a long, hot shower. She doesn't look away from the page. I ask if she wants to get ramen. She shrugs. I look at her, for traces of her. Her eyes tired from drugs, from the world's projected shame, from holding tight, salvaging her mind, her creative force. I look hard for any remnant of us. For our new tattoos and pints of beer and Billy Bragg and making love our first summer together two years before. I look for recognition, for the shapes I make myself into for her: woman, dyke, girl. I'm sorry, I say, cheeks wet with tears. For what? she asks.

What are you into? What do you have?

G, ket, speed, acid, 2cb, molly one ket two speed Danke Danke what? Okay, yeah, I'll try some first. Yeah, good shit. Fuck don't have small bills. Give me one ket four speed. Here. No don't need change, ha, a tip.

Can I get your number?

I thought this was a work party. Baby squints at the clear vials across from me. I'm crouched on the closed toilet. Her wide fingers are on my purchases: drugs, me, her, in the horror-light of a single bulb. Just cut it already. She does, calling me a gremlin. True—I wink, leaving my toilet perch. We breathe deep into the first gram. I can feel the music on the walls now. The lines of speed navigate holy, cold light through me. Someone knocks at the door. Baby adjusts her leather trousers in the mirror, looking at herself like I look at her. Her thin white T-shirt and soft red lips announce vitality and refined ease. Stupefied, I follow her out of the bathroom.

I thought this was a work party, I try again as we wade to the bar. It is—she looks at me over her shoulder—this is the photographer's apartment, but he sets it up like this once a month. What about the neighbors? She shrugs. The bar is a dining room table with several mini-fridges under it. Open bottles of wine, beers and cracked plastic cups are scattered on top. The rest of the room is people lingering. Clumps of dancing, of smoking. Then there's a doorway without a door. There's a booth and huge speakers and smoke and lasered light piercing straight until meeting the curve of someone's sweaty form.

Light doesn't turn corners like voices do, I remind myself. Then to the left is a long hallway. People sit on the floor or hotly lean, smoking. Two people in black mesh kiss slow. A guy in a suit coat and no shirt crawls to the bathroom. Someone in a white jumpsuit tries to drag her friend to the dance floor.

Baby passes me two beers. Merci. Bien sûr. She leads me to a group of artists. I remember not remembering their names but nodding at a person in all red who assured me that color was a reason to be alive. I'm going to cry, I said. I did, smiling, she was so right. I decided I could be alive. I'll wear red tomorrow—I hugged the person, feeling my heartbeat red into them. Sappy American, Baby scolded. She was between my body and the wall, now, my arm above her. I finished my second beer, looking at her, smiling, letting her watch me watch her. Another line? Bien sûr.

Here we can do it in the open. She waved to her friends and we sat down against a wall and tipped more speed onto her cracked phone screen. I thought this was a work party, I said with a laugh. It is, she said, putting up with me.

I don't want to go to the dancing part of this party, I said. Baby, taking a line, told me she didn't either. I grabbed us more beers. We did the lines. We sat, smoked. We talked to several people. I grabbed a stray skateboard for Baby to sit on and crouched across from her. Tell me something, she said. The wings of me coiled into rest as I took a big line of k. You are magic, I said. Magic, I said as I leaned forward into her chest.

Give me my board. Oh hi. Baby looked up, it was the photographer. She kind of tumbled as she got up and so I tried to help her. The photographer took the board and said something in German to Baby. She said stuff back. I kept doing lines, crouched below. The photographer seemed to not remember me, which was strange but okay. His beard had grown out a bit. It was silver and he wore his blue hood up. Have either of you seen my gallery?

We followed him out the front door. The stairs' edges were candied in orange rubber. My knees became micro-tremors. We walked down past a group of Australians with dark tattoos and tailored clothes. They seemed to be discussing some work-related topic because, as the photographer passed, they all turned quietly into their cigarettes, their beers.

We followed him into an alley: slender, spine-like: piss and shit, trash and starless sky. He unlocks a thick red door. He leads us up a wobbly spiral staircase. Baby and him erase into a dark above. He hits the lights.

Translucent red sculptures made from jagged plastic frame the white floor. This is turning me on, I think as I walk into the center of the white cube. From the corner of my eye, I see the photographer touch Baby's neck. Fuck. Not this.

Baby's sexual force was a cascade of trueness that humbled me. We respected the wild other lives we led beyond the enormous angles of care we cast for each other. Still, this hurt. We agreed early on that we wouldn't carry on full romantic relationships outside each other. Sex was sex, though, and we knew it could happen. We promised to tell each other everything or include each other. The moment sex was secret, we had actually cheated. More and more, I knew the arrangement couldn't hold for much longer.

I turned around and he was kissing her badly. What the fuck? I thought. They seemed involved in the bad kissing, so I made myself comfortable on the floor, leaning on one of the less sharp sculptures, cutting lines. He would look at me every couple seconds, as if to invite me. I watched as she felt for his cock, as he tugged at her thin white T-shirt. Maybe Baby knows about me and him in the back room. I guess I'll make directing my kink. Annoyed at Baby more than him, I said, Kiss her slower, idiot.

He and I were not equals. He was a middle-aged, tall cis guy with a massive cock. He was reckless and intense but successful and intelligent. Baby liked his photos. I knew enough from Baby and from doing the same drugs in the same rooms on the same nights that I would be ushered to join them soon enough.

I reminded myself not to compare our articulations of masculinity. I thought through the strict imperatives that belong to the fiction of gender. Cis men are not the only men, I reminded everyone and no one in my mind. The hot photographer's version of masculinity is likely an unexamined, compulsory affect. I fight for mine.

My thoughts were intercepted. I blinked back into the

room. Baby snarled some hot desire line. The photographer picked her up. I ask Baby if she's serious right now. She says nothing so I fuck off. Their rude nonissue with my existence is cue enough. I slip back into my/Dad's leather jacket. I head for the stairs. I look at them, all the red peaks surrounding them, Baby's legs bent around him. I feel not jealousy, but a sadness for his throbbing universe. No one questions if he's a man. That must be nice.

This is where I stand up tall inside myself, unraveling into trueness as I spiral down the metal stairs. In the alley I breathe deep, remembering the color red. I walked not toward the party but past. Hard, going the only way I knew to go: deeper into night.

Baby is heading to Paris for the week. She's curating a new exhibition at an old gallery. She tells me she and the photographer had some falling-out, thank god. What happened? I asked. He got possessive and competitive at work. It was too much. I thought to myself how utterly dismissive it was that he wasn't jealous of me.

Fucking prick, I said. He wanted things that she didn't want to give. Well, I'm glad you cut it off, I said. It's totally fucked you made out with him in front of me, I remind her. She looks so entirely sorry and says so.

She reminds me she was wrecked and that they didn't even have sex. She said shortly after I left she searched the party for me. I take this as a kind lie, the one meant to make me feel important. The photographer quickly slips into a forgotten fucked-up monologue that I'll probably never write.

She tells me she wants it to be just us again, our little monogamous world. I agree and hug her long. The moment angled an openness in me. The dim gray morning made me sad, steady and brave. Years of knowing the unknowable swelled up in one surge that latched to language. I want to tell you, before I go, I think I want to transition, like medically.

Yeah, I know, Baby said, not looking. She walked around

the apartment, steeping her black tea, packing and doing her makeup. Not knowing what to say next, I lay back in bed and looked at the ceiling. My heart pounded with fear. I wished my wings could show her wings the wind that brought me here.

Well, I don't know about another man in the world, she said. I laughed. She said it wasn't a joke. My core weight collected and scattered. I'm just sure now—I looked at her, propped up on my elbows. I wanna be your boyfriend. She sat on the edge of the bed and slowly told me she loved me but that she wasn't straight. I asked, What about the photographer? That was just fun, she explained, I don't want to be in a relationship with a man.

I got up to help her zip her suitcase. I'm romantically a lesbian, she said, exhaling her weight on top of her suitcase. I know, I know, I said. But just because I'm a guy doesn't mean this is a straight relationship. The zipper caught on a corner. We stopped and looked at each other, her crouched on top of the suitcase and me on the floor. I don't know what to tell you, I don't want to be with a man like that.

Air left me for several moments. She looked exhausted, vexed and holy. Despite her homoromantic clarity, I sought a protection from her. I wanted her to hold me. I wanted her to tell me that, of course, I am only becoming more myself, not someone else. I wanted to emerge from my confession with her by my side.

You mean you don't want to be with a trans man, I said.

She left in a rush, slamming a canvas in the door before

saying sorry sorry sorry and that we can talk more later. Tell me how the workshop goes, she yelled over her shoulder.

Drugs got me to my feet. I grabbed the baggies tucked inside my desk, relieved that I won't have to hide while Baby is gone. Tapping out most of the powder, I inhale deep. The sun seems smaller, my heart warmer. I lie back on the bed and have a small thought: My body could be my own.

I change into black leather trousers, Baby's creepers and a big black hoodie, avoiding my reflection. Out, I tread down Hermannstraße, feeling sad and vivid clear. I walk with a line in my head Toni had said one drunk night months before: I do not hide, I am hidden. I do not hide, I am hidden, I do not hide. With each step, I am a person in the world unhidden, someone who opens doors, who feels rain.

I turn into an open bar. Alone with drink after drink, I darken. Alone with drink after drink, I am hidden.

o

1   *

I first saw him at a gallery. I had just finished the focus of my week, the writing workshop, where we read, drank and critiqued each other in a polite circle. I showed up to the exhibition late, alone and thirsty. It was lightly raining. There was a dry Q and A with the artist about the choke hold of meaning making or whatever. I immediately noticed the unkempt fury of his dark curls. Unsure of how to approach him but knowing that I had to, I moved closer to the front of the small standing crowd. The fluorescence of the gallery made me feel twitchy and my hands, now holding two full plastic cups of bad wine, trembled a little. I situated myself just behind him and stopped listening to the artist speak. I was suddenly very aware of what I was wearing. I felt my gross, sockless feet in my busted platform Docs. I could feel the hard of me throb in my too tight, dark-wash, high-waisted denim. I regretted that my pine-colored, ankle length trench covered my ass. My impossible chest was bound, viciously, beneath a well-worn, oversized Black Flag T-shirt. I stood and chugged the free wine, wondering if he would turn around.

When the Q and A wrapped, I followed him to the bar.

How do you feel about that, I leaned his direction, pointing to an ugly orange abstract on the wall. We met eyes. Something inside me fell away. He shrugged and looked at my two glasses of wine. What's your name, I asked calmly, keeping eye contact. He seemed nervous, alone and very into his drink. I'm Gabriel, he said, offering his hand. Unable to shake his, I winked and lifted my two glasses. He asked, What's your name? Do you wanna have a cigarette with me, I responded, avoiding such a personal question. The small crowd had dispersed around the gallery and onto the narrow street.

Outside, he told me that he's also a writer. I wondered if he was any good. He told me he had dropped out of university and worked at a bar around the corner. I asked if he wanted to go there, more free alcohol looming. He said sure like he hated the idea. His mouth was the most expressive thing about his face, full and slow with each exhale of smoke, each sip of wine.

Once we started talking, everything felt precious. He only stuck around for one beer but gave me his email and phone number. He asked that I send him some of my writing. Churning in attraction, I sent him an imagined interview I wrote with Henry Miller the next day. He responded that evening with a sharp but complimentary critique. He read something others didn't in my work. His knowing seemed to permeate the lines of day-to-day. The next day he sent me an excerpt of his novel draft, a boring account of contemporary cults. I tried to think beyond the letters, I could know the depth of him that way.

When Baby got back from Paris, we remained stuck. We tried to smooth it out but my feelings of rejection, and hers of loss, were powerful. We tried to be kind to each other, trying to be the thing we needed most. Before Gabriel and I had even spoken, I knew I couldn't really tell Baby about him. My attraction flooded the reasoning she would ask me to have about it.

Gabriel was, optically, straight and cis. He occupied a kind of for-fleeting-fun-only place in our relationship. Cis, hetero men were nothing except everything that was wrong with the world. Crushing this hard on him betrayed our unspoken queer norms: the scowls that can only come from abjection. We reproduced the pain we felt. In our quick to cancel wit, there was an unspoken supremacy, ours. We unknowingly recycled hierarchical power, thinking that we were doing something new. Our categories, however, replicated the very structures we fought to survive.

The drab stucco behind Gabriel's head is a pale yellow. Thick slopes of rich blue spray paint spurt from his head. I can't make out the bulbous letters but they seem to communicate sex. Graffiti chats up every surface here: public or private. It creeps, fervent-irreverent and beautiful, on the marigold doors of the U-Bahn, on the posh façades of Charlottenburg, on gold relic statues in Hermannplatz and on every piss-soaked stall wall in every club. Try-hard new bars in Friedrichshain badly mimic it.

Bikers rush by, the convex swoosh of wheels, chains and clicking gears. Clusters of the unridden are locked on light posts, trees, gates, signs and one another. Then there's the sordid smell of dead animal, kebab, that I vomited this morning. Then there's the small dark cars and beige taxis. They exhale smog, alit in their wading lines of red brake lights. Then they're propelled forward in a white-light smear, their rubber tread smoothing cobblestone.

Gabriel would be too fucking precious in the red bar light. I see him now: his tight jeans, white mesh tank and too-big vintage, pin-striped blazer. Her wide eyes would dart to the bar. He would get up, his gunky sneakers heavy on the floor. He would come back with two pints. Her long fingers would gesture forward, ranty and gorgeous. Play that I Am Kloot song we fucked to on accident, she'd say. "Proof" or "No Fear of Falling"? Beer would evermore be on our lips. It would be slick in our brains. I'd be sticky-thick with tenderness.

That night, early into our thing, we sit at one wobbly table on the terrace of a small smoky bar on Bergmannstraße. It's a cellar, essentially, the front door takes you down a half flight of creaky stairs. The inside is hectic with red neon light, the walls are painted black and there are mirrors all over the place. It's brimmed in smoke. Groups of cool people lean and chat and wrap their tattooed arms around each other. The bartender lets me do blow on the counter as long as I share. Like everyone else in this city, he's a DJ.

I look at Gabriel, who somehow hasn't finished his shots yet. I reach across and take one of his and he smiles. I meet his gaze. Something is happening to me, I know then. I'm washed with clarity. He looks prettily at me, suspending me in affection. I breathe in the hot tugging weight between us.

My blood chimes in the syncopated notes of my heart. Some deep part of me falls to my stomach in a colossal note. A vibrational sureness pulses in the cock-crux of me. What is happening to me? I love this song, Gabriel says, let's go inside.

As I nervously hold the door for him, he passes with his empty pint, giving me his last shot of tequila. I dumbly tilt the warmth back and follow him down the stairs, onto two open barstools. My hands tremble like they do in the mornings, but these shakes are different, they're just nerves.

From the inside pocket of my leather jacket, I manage to pull out two vials, a razor blade and a twenty-euro bill. Gabriel looks around the bar. The bartender turns up New Order. I don't remember which is which, I say with a smile, eyeing the two plastic vials. I gum them both and get numb from the second but not the first. One of each for me, please, this one is the blow, I say, the other is K. Gabriel's cuts are thick, gorgeous banks of snow. I find myself staring at him too long. This is Gabriel. I nod at the bartender. The bartender lights a smoke: Hey, man.

Like the first drink of the day, the burn in my nose soothes. Another shot, two inches of tequila with a slice of orange. The bartender asks where Baby is and I shrug. Gabriel leans his head on my shoulder and I touch his leg. I gulp. You drink like me, he whispers. Lighting a cigarette and lifting his head. How do you drink? Like my life depends on it, he says, laughing in one light exhale. We talk about my writing workshop.

He goes on about how age will fuck us all and Frank O'Hara's punctuation.

The bar eventually fills and then empties and we finish the blow. As Gabriel and I wander into night, I think about taking his hand.

At the front door of my building, Gabriel wraps his arms around me. He smells like the best cigarette I've ever smoked. I kiss him firstly on the neck, then his mouth, but I'm chalk-dry. I've bitten through my cheek. Still, he holds the side of my neck with a generative grip. It takes every tense cell of me not to write a poem with our bodies right there. He asks if he can come in. I have a girlfriend, I whisper as if it were a secret, as if it were myth. Let's go to yours. I smile. Can't. He laughs, shaking his head. I've got a girlfriend too.

○

2   *

Gabriel's taking out the cash we need to pick up. His legs are firm in his black jeans. His worn white sneakers are pleasantly large, and his thick knit red sweater makes me want to stick my face between his shoulder blades and ride on top wherever he goes.

The ATM flashes green, then blue, and people with short bangs in all black, angled clothes and tattoos pass us. He slings his arm over my shoulder as we turn to the street: Call the guy? I tell him I already did, and we walk back to his studio. He tells me about his life in France, about his unfinished degree in architecture. He explains shyly that he might like to be seen as a woman sometimes. I can see that, I say, meeting his eyes and seeing her. He asks me about Iowa, and I begin and end with the sky.

We're being idiots. We drink vodka mate after vodka mate and face each other on either side of the tiny coffee table. We smoke cigarette after cigarette and take turns playing music. His room is crowded with books, records and stacks of marked-up papers. There's one black leather swivel chair, a desk and a small mattress in one corner.

Empty green beer bottles are everywhere. A shared kitchen and bathroom are down a narrow hallway. There isn't an overhead light, just one vintage lamp in the corner with a blue bulb. It's grimy, bare and comfortable. He doesn't ask me to take off my boots.

I joked about the bend in his wrists and he joked about my high voice. Our faces got really close as he whispered, You're really *such* a gay boy, aren't you? Thank you for noticing, I smirked, ecstatic. I felt something lift then, some curated part of my personality fell away and words for myself didn't matter anymore. There I was: a gay boy, felt and true in relational calm. A moment of rare stillness followed. The painter in the room next door dropped something. Getting up to smoke at the window, I joked, Or maybe I'm straight. I said it tentatively and with a warm smile. She looked away and so we moved on.

When the guy calls, I go outside and get in his car and ask for one and nod: Danke. I wink at him because I don't know how to say you smell good in German. He smiles and drives me to the corner and I get out, all rushy and in deep with Gabriel. My love is true in its expansive ability to spread to others.

With the energy of childhood's light, I walk back to his office with my tread hovering slightly above the pavement. I touch the vials in the tight denim of my front left pocket, knowing, then, that I loved him. Baby came to mind and I flashed in shame. I pushed forward, knowing this mess was of my own making. Baby could never know. I'd protect her from this.

Later that night, I tried to show Gabriel my love with my legs wrapped around him. In the disorderly magic of our touching, he said, You're *such* a pretty boy. I held the smooth wet stone of his shoulders. I felt his breath on me, his bites on my neck. Overwhelmed in sensation, I ferally pleaded: Don't stop. Making the cold floor hot, I healed in the precious, core sensation we made together. I could feel all of him. I could breathe. He listened with his whole body, thrusting dreams back inside me forever.

You've got to go, he said at four a.m. I was looking out the window with him, smoking. My head was on his shoulder, the cold air felt good. I felt satisfied, exhausted and near. I thought he was joking. He wasn't. His girlfriend had called something like twelve times. He walked me to the U-Bahn at Kottbusser Tor. I slung my arm around him as my legs trembled from the cold, from the drugs, from the love we made. As I descended the stairs, I looked back and watched him jogging home to her.

○

3 *

I go to my desk. It's wedged between my library and the rolls of canvas, turpentine, charcoal and paintbrushes. I take more speed and consider how perfectly melancholy Gabriel was, sitting across from me in his room, reading something I didn't like. How tender his mouth. How sweet his smile. The tattoo of a red snake on his left forearm snuck out from his sleeve. I think over the way his brief kiss goodbye last night made me throb. I decide it doesn't matter if I don't like his prose. He summons all these new words in me. We keep messaging.

Me:

Pulsality (noun)

1. To be so wide-eyed and rolling in the delectation of your entire living that it throbs through you in cock, in cunt, in blood, in heart, in fist, in step

2. The hypomanic bliss of the bipolar and the chronically depressed

     Gabriel:

Let's feel that together sometime

Me:

I'm a folded heart open in the velocity of change

Longer, longer still white lines

Wavering in turbulence of city

I walk with your cock hard in my mind

Me:

I want my voice to be an extension of your bedroom

But king-sized and sexed not queen and alone

      Gabriel:

Want to meet soon? Alone at my place now.

    I chuck my red notebook, inky pen, four Berliner Pilsners, a fresh pack of camels and a hoodie into my backpack. The vials of speed stay in my jacket and I jut to the Landwehr-kanal, thinking I'd walk through any threshold Gabriel is on the other side of.

o

4   *

At midday I leave Baby asleep and shower. I drink three mugs of coffee and have my guy deliver more speed. The money I didn't earn is running low, naturally. Too scared to see the remaining balance, I assure myself I will look tomorrow and plan my life accordingly. When Baby gets up, I'm cutting a line. I ask: You want? No, yes, no, okay. Baby leans over my lap to the table. Where were you last night? she asks, turning on the kettle. Met up with some writers, I say, Gabriel looked over my new story. I'd told Baby that Gabriel was my best editor, which wasn't untrue.

We go to the Hinterhof. Baby shows me her latest. She tells me we need time together, just us. I nod. She asks me where I am. These are beautiful, I say, and put my phone away.

Baby had been pouring thick layers of hot wax on her massive colorscapes. Once the wax dried, she'd carve lines into it with her butterfly knife, making rivers of color beneath the wax. We walk around, looking from every angle as they drip.

o

5   *

What time do we really ever have? Something massive is happening to me. Some entirety is taking place. I feel Gabriel fill
my mind, even when he's not here. Each corner I turn, I feel
his hands, see his smile. Each step I take belongs in his direction. I get good on speed and whiskey and message him about
the dream, that erotic pinnacle. In my sleeping life, Gabriel
pins me to a cold wall in the room where I have workshop. His
touch feels enormous, it makes the wall fall away. Then we
are floating in flat dark space; we orbit orange planets, kissing.

o

6 *

Gabriel's spunk is on my boxers. That's what he calls it. I like
to say cum. As in fill me up, as in breed me. He stood over
me and got it on my face. I think it's hilarious and weird and
boyish. Before we walked to Templehof, I asked why the fuck
he Jackson Pollocked me that way. He said it's about trust.
I laughed at him wholly for the first time. He said fuck off,
embarrassed. Then he smiled shyly. I knew that we could see
the idiocies of each other as frank and sweet. I could tell him
anything.

We sat in Templehof and the sun ate away our hangover. I
thought about how this park isn't a park at all but Hitler's for-
mer airfield. There's something ghostly about Berlin: a massive vacancy in me as I walk. I can feel histories, versions
of myself in Weimar before the book burning of '33. I would
have been wearing black, dancing late, dreaming wide for the
first time. With Hirschfeld's research, we began to let pathol-
ogy go its own way—we take another drink and touch the
honest, contemplative forms of each other.

Us trans people, us queers, we made it here somehow. Berlin, our vague refuge. We sync with the imagined shapes of

those like us who came before. In Berlin, we party and fuck as if, finally, we might breathe in our bombed-out mecca for an evening and not fear death or his slower cruelties, punishment and shame.

Gabriel reads something he loves aloud, a poem. I lay in the curve of his arm and worried our girlfriends would catch us.

o

7 *

Gabriel's author photo sucks. So does mine. The poster, for the reading tonight, is on my desk. I open a beer, click the Facebook event and scroll through the list of people attending.

I wear a huge blue-striped button-down, perfectly creased from sleep, scuffed vintage Frye boots and a red beanie. Baby promised she'd be there but I doubt she'll be done at the gallery in time. A gold inverted cross dangles from my left ear. I slide orange glitter onto my eyelids. I do several lines. I grab the stack of stories I named *Novel*, open a beer for the road and head to war.

The train drags me to Gabriel, my hidden, my kept one. I feel the ache of tears nagging. No one can see us. No one will see us as I stand and read about us to everyone. Us, for me to know and for Gabriel to ignore. I listen to Jesus and Mary Chain and breathe through the rapid, heavy knocks of my heart.

Out of the train, my tread is over worn cobblestone, cigarettes, bottle caps and oily Döner foil angled in creases and in light. The heat of summer has calmed into a late autumn

cool. Each person I pass could be him or could be Baby find-
ing me out. My chest binder hurts. I try another useless
attempt at a full breath. Futility is necessary. There are no
means to my ends.

I turn the corner to the venue, a sterile room for readings,
for workshops. I invited Gabriel to come and read some of
his novel as a guest in the workshop. He and his girlfriend
are just left of the front door, smoking and nodding. She has
a small frame, long straight blonde hair, cool thick sneakers
and a black dress. Gabriel told me once, pushing down from
above: I like to hold you like this.

Knowing he can feel me wanting him above me, I scan the
clusters of people. Every bit of me plays atomic. Against all
sense, I walk up and say hi. Gabriel seems scared but says
hello. He looks at her. She tells me she's excited to hear me
read, she tells me Gabriel likes my stuff. You do? I joke, meeting his eyes. Ha—he shrugs. Do either of you need a beer? I
ask clumsily. She holds her full bottle up and smiles at me.
Gabriel looks away as he puts his arm over her shoulders. See
ya inside, he says. I cringe and open the door.

In the bathroom, I allow slow, warm tears. I rummage
through the burdens of my affection. After over a month of
loving in secret, I wish I could undo myself from him. I cut
a line to remind myself I'm here to read. I keep the orange
glitter flecks from my tears on my cheeks and leave the stall.

Gabriel's girlfriend is washing her hands. Hey, I say.
Gabriel said you might have some . . . she begins shyly. You
want a line? I ask, quickly wiping a tear and sniffling. She
nods and I step back into the stall and cut one for her, two

for me. This is weird, I think briefly. You're gorgeous, I tell
her, the surge in my nose. She rolls her eyes and slowly
takes a third of the line. She leans her head back, as if that
does anything. I finish her line, gum the rest and look at
our shoes.

Do you think Gabriel is sleeping with someone? she asks,
as if it's a joke. She puts her beer on the sticky stall floor
and ties up her hair. How is she this comfortable with me?
Gabriel says I'm paranoid. I've been suspicious for, like, a
couple weeks now and he told me I could ask you about it
because you may help settle my fears, since you're, like, his
good friend. She continues awkwardly, And ya know, you and
Baby are, well, you're gay. So is your boyfriend, I think to
myself.

I can't look up from my boots on the tile. I try to breathe.
All I could muster to say was, I know he cares for you. I
looked up and she looked for my eyes.

She asked, annoyingly astounded, Have you been crying?
Yeah—I nodded. She seemed genuine. I liked her. She asked,
What's wrong? I'm in love, I admitted, and tried to move past
her. She hugged me forcefully. Her neck smelled like sage, I
could feel her rabbit pulse. We left the bathroom together and
waded to the bar. She got me a beer. Thanks, I said. She said,
Hang in there. I noticed my orange glitter flecks on her neck,
perfect.

I take my seat in the front row next to Gabriel. My arm
touches his as I sit down. Your girlfriend talked to me, I
whispered. Good, I told her to. You're a fucking asshole, I
nervously say, making me lie like that. He doesn't look at me

and says, She didn't try and kiss you, did she? What, no, I said, feeling emptier than before. She told me she finds you cute, he adds, she might have a crush. I ask if we should all fuck in the bathroom later. That's not funny, he scolds. What are you going to read? I ask. He holds a stack of paper up, not looking at me.

o

8   *

The bar was tiny, it only had two tables. The walls and ceiling were red, the décor glistened. The woman at the bar liked him a lot, winking and talking about Bruce Springsteen in my direction. He looked like this was the last time. I feared it with agony. I tried to keep up with him. We talked about Keats's poem "This Living Hand." I sank into his eyes and told him the boy truth of me.

That makes sense, you've always felt so boy to me, he said. Between us I felt an unopened excitement, possible lives together, the one he knew I wanted with him. Like he was sorry, he said he and Charlotte were going to therapy, that they were going to try to work it out. Oh, I said, too smashed with shock to react.

I tried not to feel all the way but my eyes glossed over with tears. He paid for the beers. On the street, he looked at me too long and said, You'd be a really good boyfriend. The knife twisted. We kissed. He brought the inside of his hand over my skull and then held it firm on the back of my neck, protecting something we shared. Good night, he said. As I watched him become shadow, I became a cascade of sinking need. To Gabriel, I became superfluous. To myself, I became silent in loss.

Desolate, I turned back into the bar. I made myself vomit in the bathroom. I slowly washed my hands and avoided my reflection. I did what I knew to do and ordered another drink.

*

*

*

*

A remembered shiver of a night alone,
Making love with Gabriel

We stand on planet balcony in
Solar-system-him-and-I

We waver upwards as the snow comes down
Do you feel guilty, I asked

No,

I feel like you're hurtling me towards the sky, he said with a smile
Conviction warmed me as I took a long drag
I said   I love you

He said   no,

           You don't

                I teared up, looking for his eyes

                Icy gusts thinned his smoke

He just   looked at me   and

  Finally   he   said

                You're just   so   beautiful

                    He   said it

                    Like   it

                    Hurt   him

o

9   *

The bench outside of Markthalle is cold. I guess what I mean is, I often feel alone with you. Gabriel uses the Gang of Four record I just bought for him to block the sun that won't set. I say me too but it's okay. We are always already so much an island, but look, I'd like to rub shores with you. Our tides, our froth, our salt. Do you like this cliff better? Or do you prefer my ocean brisk on your shallow?

You're always fucked up, it's boring, he says, squinting. How are you and Charlotte? Good, he says curtly. I feel the vial in my pocket and try to avoid a rushing necessity to order a pint at the bar adjacent to us, to beeline to the bathroom and finish this gram so that there aren't any more drugs at all, ever, anymore. Gabriel sees my mind go. The need for substance as clear as breath, as sex. I'm sorry, I say. It's just— I know. He stops me with his hand on my knee. As he gets up he flatly jokes: Just, please don't die.

Hey, wait, I try. But he walks away with *Entertainment!* slicing the sun in his grip.

I don't follow. I choose worship, although it's not much of a choice at all. I sit at the dark church of the bar and drink for the both of us. When I wake up the next afternoon, I'm pruned and miserable. Low with loss, with inaction. It's foggy. I remember hitting my head and look for evidence. I try to remember how I got home and close the curtains, light a cig.

Baby left me a note in faint pencil on a torn piece of canvas: *I found you in the hall. You hit your head, not too bad. I took off your binder for you. Take your meds. Please rest today and I'll make us dinner, idiot.* I walk to the kitchen and take a beer from the fridge.

I take a long shower, letting the steam be my everything. I use lavender bar soap and Baby's expensive face scrub. I wedge into a binder and Gabriel's worn in black T-shirt. I return to bed. I open my phone and everything sinks into a wound.

A message from Gabriel, he's going to stop seeing me, he needs to really work it out with Charlotte, he doesn't want me to contact him anymore.

I get frantic, knowing I could be perfect for him if I weren't so much myself. I start to type my reply, the panic drenching me. The chat colors turned gray. My message sends but isn't read. I click on his profile and it says, "add friend."

I stumble to the damp bathroom and vomit a burning swell of beer. I brush my teeth, chuck cold water on my face and look at myself. I can't stand the nothing that I am. I cut myself a line, grab a beer and get on my bike. Stupid with my wet hair, I ride aimlessly, thinking his name over and over. I stand up and pedal as chilly winds, all the way from the Baltic Sea, dry my tears.

After my sorrow ride, I sleep until evening and go out before Baby can stop me.

o

10 *

Wholeness is the enemy, if I must name one. The silence he cracks is violent. All the bends of him I want around me.

Remembering, with ache, the park, that sunny one. Gabriel and I met some of his friends, including a couple and their kid. I watched him cutely engage with the six-year-old, singing something soft in German that I'd never heard before. I watched him, smiled, drank his beers and smoked. I was made enormous in unavoidable, terrifying love.

Which note did he leave off on and when was the last time he asked me to lay my body on his? I listen for something as expansive as his eyes—all I see in the chat are the detestable ellipses each period bounces in gray, then dissolves. Which company do you keep, if not mine? Which balconies do you stare out from, if not mine? Each protracted day aches in the without-you cast. It's almost winter.

Now each turn away casts me true. Truer. Beginning as if it's the end. It is. It's not wanting to get here that got me here. It's my stern avoidance of being known that made me see-able. I couldn't meet the world's gaze. I stayed soaked in cities and big loss and couches, always a coffee table with our array, white lines and bottles and stacked books, candles and dying flowers.

A whole dizzy city of people standing, looking cool like they aren't looking at all. It was all one evening that smudged into years. Fortified by imagined company and lost love. Clusters of us, my fellow death stars, going out with our windows down. Berlin held a vibrating tenacity. I was exhaling tears in the backseat of a creamy Mercedes taxi, blinking at the Spree's persistent blur, looking for a way out.

From the taxi, I approach the dark fact before me: Berghain's authoritarian façade. I am haunted, thinking: Let me in, let me in, let me in.

The room can't be any other. It's this archy bend of a space: one corner of Berghain. A smoking landing, perhaps. It's this mezzanine I climb to as I come down. Predictable, in its furnishings, sticky leather couches, ottomans turned fucking platform, turned perfect place for me to extend wings wide and smoke.

It's the living openness of partying that hurts me. The self-calculated, arranged arrival and departure of my life. Is it durational if it never ends? Yes. I end. Cigarettes and I and lines and bottles and the trying flex of kiss all try to end me, I'm trying to end me. I'm passive, abject and living close to death, passing it off as fun.

I am looking far, far off somewhere, lying in the sweaty fogged den of what is essentially the break room of Berghain. Everyone looks cool, I remember thinking. People in fishnets and latex body suits and guys in leather straps. The house music hurts. I wore tight blue overalls and dirty Airforce 1s and nothing else. I was trying to let myself feel denim and chest with nothing in between. I was trying to pretend I had a flat chest. My white T-shirt hung from my back pocket.

I liked seeing people have sex, only ever feeling worried when I saw a woman bent over with two guys taking turns on a balcony at Kit Kat one night. I was wearing more than anyone around me. Is she okay? I looked up to her on the balcony and searched for her eyes. Our glances met. She smiled at me, all feral and cruel.

It's okay to ache like this. I ache alone like this in these clubs full of others, feeling like one of many others' aches.

The smoking room was a stop to make, a dream to sink into. A checkpoint in the vibrating limestone warehouse, this hedonist monolith. As I lay there, melted and docile but buzzing true from the ketamine, from the blow, I charted a plan for myself. The room was changing hue, a dragging incomprehensible light from dawn came in. One more smoke, one more line, then the walk home.

Then there was the person across from me: He looked exactly like Gabriel. He had messy, dark hair. She wore a large thin black T-shirt with holes and bleach stains that fell to her upper thighs. As he returned the smile, she leaned to her back and put her legs up. He slowly undid his boots. She turned back to face me. There was a meter between us. I lost my map for the way home. Home didn't matter at all anymore.

I opened my mouth as if to say: Let's spend all the time we have left alive together. Just as my lips parted, she got up and walked toward me. Thick, glossy raven wings flashed from her back and disappeared as quickly as they emerged.

She took my badly rolled cigarette, standing with one leg between my legs and the other on the outside of my frame. You look exactly like this guy I know, I said.

He smiled and bent down to kiss my neck. I touched up his inner thigh. In my ear, she whispered: "Become what you are."

Her words chilled my skin as memory traces of Gabriel grazed me.

With that, she kissed my forehead and grabbed her boots by the laces. Her wings remained tucked as she descended from the mezzanine. My cigarette was on her lips as she went back into the clogged revelry of sweating bodies.

On my stark walk home I found the first email from Gabriel. He had sent notes on my writing and a Nick Cave song called "Jubilee Street." I put in my headphones. The blank horizontal of the drugs wearing thin turned gorgeous and thick with Nick Cave's sediment voice.

I draft an email I know I can't send: Hey, fuck you. I just met some winged version of you. Jubilee Street is you inside me now, forever.

There was nothing I could do but become the painful nothing Gabriel made us. Sometimes, late at night, I'd want to tell Baby everything. For her to hold me and my broken heart. I nearly did, one time. Baby faced her canvas. I cast a clip lamp in my right hand for her. I looked at the bottle in my left hand with torment. Baby asked what was so wrong with me lately. She wanted to know why I was in bed so much, why I wasn't helping Gabriel with his novel edits. Fuck that guy, I managed to say with stability. What happened? Baby looked at me, her massive, gorgeous eyes too good for the lost sight of me, she pulled paintbrush off canvas. I brought the light down and told her: It's fucked, he just stopped talking to me altogether. Baby smirked. What an idiot, she said, shaking her head like this was all inevitable.

I handed her the clip light and got myself another beer. I never liked his writing anyway, Baby said. Plus, I heard he's fucking another writer and his girlfriend doesn't even know. I hit my head on the fridge door and asked, Where did you hear that? I don't know—she shrugged—think it was the Australian poet. The one with the motorcycle. Baby stepped back to see her painting from farther away. It was smears of cobalt and layers of charcoal shapes that looked like a blueprint.

She laughed: He probably stopped talking to you 'cause he's busy leading a double life.

Read me something, she said. I don't have anything right now, I said as I thought about all the fuck poems about Gabriel on my computer. Just read me something that makes you feel your feet on the ground, here, tonight, with me. Her kindness made me hurt more. I found the thick Elizabeth Jennings anthology that Gabriel softly handed me one afternoon. Heavy in my left hand, I read the poem Gabriel marked for me, "Is It Dual Natured?" and in my right hand I cast the light for Baby.

As days bled on, I knew with devastating clarity that Gabriel had tucked me into silence for good—I was made a ghost by a ghost. This wordless, faceless rejection left me looking blankly for myself in the mirror, biting my cuticles until they bled, fantasizing about giving my body to men to smear with their hate, drinking more than ever, using more than ever. I'd tell Baby to stop worrying, as she'd asked me what I was taking. Her persistent care made my rage unravel.

Just leave me alone, I said, getting into jeans. Where are you going, you idiot? Baby was angry but kept her cool all the same. I could sense her sadness just there, under the surface of her words. I met her eyes for a rare second and wanted to exhale everything there, between us. I wanted to tell her about Gabriel, wanted her to slap my stupid face, to spit on me, to kick me out. I needed her to make physical all the pain I caused her. She looked at the door then and darted to put herself between me and the rest of my night. Get out of the way, I said with a grin. You have to stop. Baby pushed me back. Baby, don't be like this, let me go out. I looked at her magenta crew socks, the oversized Iowa T-shirt she slept in, the slow tears on her cheeks.

I couldn't venture true articulation, it'd break me. Cruelty kept me moving. You're sick, I told her, and tried again to open the door. You're the most selfish person I've ever known, she said with wide truth. Caught in her words, I stammered for something to say.

Good, I finally said, I'll fuck off. Her eyes found mine for a second, but I pushed through her and the door, hard.

The sun is coming up and I don't know how it keeps doing that. I'm sitting on the cold sidewalk in front of our building, just to the right of the door. My back leans on the façade below the buzzer I can't reach. I did too much ketamine again and can't move, my limbs heavy and useless. I tap my pockets again for my key. I feel the same nothing. I managed to heft my body up to the buzzer two times but Baby hasn't answered. I stay on the sidewalk and call her again on my phone. Nothing.

I've been here long enough to not know how long I've been here. Our narrow street has large, thick old doors and shallow sidewalks. So, I've been here, trying to read my phone screen, avoiding the people who ask, "Kann ich Ihnen helfen?" as they pass.

There's vomit on my left that I ignore. As I slowly venture to the buzzer again, I hear an alert on my phone. Like moving through lava, I lift the screen to my face and see it's Gabriel. I gasp on my numbed-out perch. I squint, making out his letters. He wants to meet tonight to talk. Fuck, I think, and let my arm go limp in my lap. I tilt my chin up to the brightening sky and close my eyes. I swallow. Just as I try to fall into another fake sleep, I hear the large front door swing open.

What the fuck, Pony? It's Baby. Hi, I manage to say. She

takes the beer from my hand and hoists me up so I can lean on her side. Just too much ket. I smiled, trying to pass this all off as regular fun.

Yeah, yeah, she said, let's get you upstairs. You can't do k like blow, she scolded as she slowly lugged me up. When will it pass? I asked. She sat me on the edge of the bed and took off my bomber jacket slightly graced with vomit, my boots, my dusty trousers. As I sank into the bed's warmth, Baby put a heating pad around my feet and tilted warm tea into my mouth. When will it pass? I asked again, still unable to move. I don't know, Baby said, getting up and picking up her backpack to leave again, I don't know.

I wake up and it's evening again. I can move now. I tried to say no to Gabriel but showered and got ready to meet. My arms on either side of the porcelain sink, I looked at myself. I felt my cock. I knew my scowl true. I didn't know how much longer I could sustain my own breath. Putting orange glitter on my eyelids, I decided to pick up some blow before meeting Gabriel. Thanks for helping me, I text Baby. Sure, I'll see you later, she replies.

His eyes kill me. He's across the bar table. We're really risk-
ing it, going to my and Baby's spot like this. He looks nervous
but remains polite. He makes comments about the interior,
about his new favorite Elizabeth Jennings poem. You look
really good, I said. He did. He wore a thin black T-shirt and
black jeans. His dirty white sneakers were getting better and
better with more of the city on them. I wore dark green glit-
tery trousers and a Harley T-shirt. I noticed a small silver
chain on his neck. A charm in a C-shape was barely visible
from under the thin cotton of his shirt.

Is that necklace for Charlotte? He looked down. Oh yeah.
We both took long gulps then. His eyes kept darting around
the bar, uneasy and wound tight. You're still in love with her,
I take it. That's why, well, one of the reasons why I wanted
to meet. Terror wheeled over me and I reached for his leg
under the table for stability. We're engaged, I mean, it's for
visa stuff, of course, but also, like, for each other. I slid my
hand off his leg and leaned back in my chair. Why are you
telling me this?

He looked at his beer before leaning in, trying to find my
eyes. I care about you, he said. I'm worried for you. Shut
the fuck up. I rolled my eyes, finishing my beer. My terror

quickly fired into rage. Look, we have something, he said.
I know that, it's just not something you want, I shot back. I
lightly held up my empty glass and motioned to the server for
another. I felt lucky to even be across from him, which made
me even madder. Well, if you think I care about the marriage,
I don't, I said. Before he could reply, I went on, I don't kink
shame, Gabriel! Go get "Credit in the Straight World." He
tried to laugh, but I knew he saw my pain.

A fresh beer arrived and I was momentarily smoothed
over. I drank and met Gabriel's eyes. I don't think you know
how much this all means to me, I said. He reached for my
hand on the sticky table. Every inch of the bar was lit with
long candlesticks. There were fresh lilies on every table. Sullen, he said he was sorry.

As I took Gabriel's last cig, I felt a mood shift. A serious-
ness fell over him. We watched the people around us, clusters of actual Berliners living their actual evenings in actual
amber light and actual smoke. I thought of the neon in the
States, the vape clouds, the processed dead-animal meals and
the stifling smiles of customer service. I hoped Gabriel would
come back with me one day. Married or otherwise.

Let's run to the bathroom. I stood up and saw Gabriel
shake his head no. Idiot, I thought as I wistfully ashed in his
direction and turned the corner to the bathroom.

The disgusting darkness met me with care. I kept the light
off and felt for my vial before slamming my fist on the tile
counter, squatting down and gasping for Gabriel like air. I
didn't know how to know anymore. One forming future flattened into Gabriel, married. I wondered if she'd ever know

about me. If I could be real to anyone in Gabriel's life, if I ever was. I felt the massive light that Gabriel left me in, the "sun's overspill" from that Jennings poem. I felt the time he told me he wanted a place with me.

When I swung back to the table, pulsing true, my body stopped. A chair was pulled up to the table and Gabriel stood talking to Baby. Pony! Don't freak out, it's okay. Come here. Baby looked fresh, unbothered, and stunningly beautiful. Not knowing what to say, my heartbeat so fast it became one snapping vibration, I said, *What*, under my breath.

I sat down. Chugged politely, remembering Baby. I looked for their next move. We are worried about you, Baby said. I looked at Gabriel with distaste—he didn't tell her about us, he couldn't have. Baby went on, I called Gabriel, Pony. Being your friend, he's worried too. He's not my friend, I said. I looked to Baby then. You don't need to worry. I knew she contacted Gabriel because, distance aside, he was the only other person I really knew. The server came by and I ordered another beer and one for Baby.

Gabriel shuffled like it was his turn to speak. He said, I know we got fucked up together, but you went further and it was bad. Bad? I said. Well, that's a blatantly normative critique, but I guess that's what to expect from a fucking breeder like you. Baby looked at Gabriel sweetly. You're having a kid? Basically, I said.

Look, Pony, we want you to know we love you but we can't enable your use anymore. What does that mean? I asked drably, touching the precious vial in my pocket. All of me sank like grains of sand. We agreed we won't use or drink with you anymore. I laughed as the server put our drinks down. Gabriel said he was sorry, but he had to run, his eyes still darting around in fear. He and Baby hugged which hit me in a mad guilty surge, a new depth of pain.

I looked at him and said, Good intervention. With my eyes, I tried to hold him in my unalterable truth: I love you. Goodbye, he said choppily. It sounded like he really meant it.

Baby took my hand, re-tethering me to the sick reality of my life. I get it, I said. I get it. I'm not going to stop, though, you know that. This is gonna make it worse, I said. Okay— Baby nodded—just come home soon. She slid her fresh pint across the table to me and left.

I drank every beer and got a bottle of whiskey on my way home. I'm gone, far gone. I pace, because if I stop moving, the thousand suns in my chest will burn into a single fiery scream. Grief haunted by Gabriel. Dread haunted by Baby, by my cruelty, her hands open. Core-haunted, knowing the truth boy of me is true even if only Gabriel can see it. Baby stirs, so I head outside, to the balcony.

Everything I could ever know is on the thin metal barrier of this balcony. Left alone, numb. Not recent in form but in my witnesshood: my dumb sneakers and cock intelligence here, on it. The very thing once shoved into tender memory watching snow fall with Gabriel. Banks of it already melting in our noses. He went, Looks like bird carcasses. I went, Looks like you shook a worldly duvet. Looks like. Looks like. On we went.

The balcony, too close to cement for my affectionate flop over, a delectation antithetical to living. My own means to end: to vindicate myself with gravity. Smack. I blink. Never alone, even in suicide.

What is breath but a violent expenditure: I heard the froth of each exhale, the foam: salt-stale ocean of Étretat sloshed in my right inner ear. It made it inside after I touched all of me on the cliff. The mug of the cracked cold English Channel, uproarious and dramatic. Let's swim now. I looked out, far, far departed from myself. I oozed slick on my hands.

I open my ankles farther, my free hand in my dry mouth. I feel my self grow. The cliffs love you, I whisper, and let my bare back scrape the rock altar. Tu souffres de quoi? My voice streams right from the hard of my self. J/e sais que tu souffres. J/e veux nager. On y vas. Bah quand j/e parle francais chui libre, j/e pense pas des voix originales. J/e dit j/e, pas je, comme Monique Wittig m'a montré.

I take another smoke. It's just something long for my lips to see. I've lost it again, what is this thing? I shrug back at myself: epistemological scaffolding question mark comma space blink I feel Dora this morning not Freud's question mark closed parenthetical but my Dora my own scowl. See? I don't hate people, I hate the politically allocated fictions that suffocate.

I'm not a woman. I'm not American, but hear me talk about Iowa. I am not bipolar or chronically depressed, but feel the plastic conversation of state-issued pills in my pocket. I'm not, and that's how Romanticism started, Blake and Sidney lying around and writing poems with their cocks. Bodies do write poems. I've written them myself.

The "I am not this" of Romanticism is not so powerful a premise. It's blank. The usher for the rhetorical "if-then" clause showed us our seats. We watch. I watch, not in plush red but in shoes my dad bought me two years ago. The sole, another sphere that sinks me closer to my chosen cobblestone. I have a sip of wine and know it in my throat as desert. The one my Mom suffered for all of us each moment she said, I have a migraine. Another door closes.

I do not choose to dwell in thresholds. I walk in and out and back and through and over and wide-stepped or crawling: I do move. My legs cross as my anchor, my pulse reading the ancient clenches that made poetry.

Bare-handed language and I carve out of each old hall-dark dwelling. It's dark but there's always sky and always somewhere that isn't Berlin. I fold into these days, lost ones, of poem gust and "self-incurred minority" (Kant footnote here). No envelope holds the gravity of my mind's certain unknowing: all I have is this writing and a room and me: whatever fractured cancellation I summon for identity, it's still some kind of me.

I want to extinguish my own life. I'm vacant except for my need to end what has already expired: my living. But tonight. This wobbly morning: look, I'm erect in emptiness, face to the falsetto pastel of this very 05:58 sky. I look at the vial of blow and feel my body go, Yes. I take another smoke.

The next day, I put on one of Baby's dresses. It's a long, straight-line black silk slip. I put it on over my thin white Van Morrison T-shirt and look in the mirror. I read myself as femmeboy, gender fuck, man in a dress. I know I'll be read as an unhinged cis girl in a slip dress and decide it doesn't matter if no one gets my subversive exuberance because I don't miss it. I don't quell it anymore.

Before I know it I'm in the all-night bar's fluorescent bathroom, bent over. The silk of Baby's dress is pushed up to show legs, thigh, ass. I see his cobalt-blue hoodie tied at his waist. I feel the slow anxiety and earnestness of alcohol and blow. I feel the photographer's hands on my hips. Blinking back into life, I put my hands on the tile in front of me and try to get up. Let me up, I say, my body feeling heavy. I looked back at him, to see his face as if for the first time. He smiled and said, Down. He held me in place with his right hand, and with his left reached his key with a bump to my nose.

As I closed my eyes to inhale, I felt a brief reprieve, a minty coolness chased with chemical burn. I could feel God's water soothe the fire in my core. Then I sharply gasped. He shoved inside of me. Not wanting him at all, I said, Stop, trying to look back at him. His force was like my ultimate authority, drugs.

I went far, far off somewhere, staring into the grimy tile floor. Other than a twinge of pressure-pain that settled into me like a chronic diagnosis, I felt nothing. I sensed his breath and his hips. Then I felt his hand in my hair. He pulled my head back and up with his scalp grip. I looked back down, the opposite way he was pulling me, and noticed the abandoned condom on the floor by his feet. Get off me, I tried. The pop music of the bar smothered me. He thrusted at a sinister velocity, and I, enormous in hate, wanted the end. I tried to squirm free, a fish again, caught.

He adjusted his grip on my hair and pushed the side of my face onto the cold tile, craning my neck as his idiocy pushed harder into me. He hurt, fucking dreams and breath out of me forever.

When he stopped, I fell back into my breath. He quickly angled out of the bathroom and I was alone. I held my right cheek with my left hand.

I got up, pushed my hair down, and adjusted my/Dad's leather jacket. I felt what he left inside of me with silent terror. I breathed deep for a moment and then remembered the door was unlocked. I frantically moved to lock it. It flung open at me, and Baby's wide eyes looked me over. What the fuck? I could feel her anger churn atomic. Baby, no. I shook my head. Baby, please listen. Him? she asked. Seized with calamity, I tried, No, no, Baby I didn't even want to.

She stepped back into the doorway, looking me up and down. What about us? Our world? I didn't want to, I pleaded, remembering our monogamy vow with regret. She noticed the condom. Your life is disgusting, she said before swinging out of my hell. Too consumed with fear to chase, to explain, I peed and waited for more of him to come out, slowly crying. I threw away the condom and its shiny light blue wrapper. I fixed myself with a line, wiping my tears, noticing I'm almost out.

I smooth over my bound chest, focusing on how the silk

feels. The glitter from my eyelids has been almost entirely winced away. I blink. I'm blank to myself in my reflection. The bad music keeps playing. Another person yells. Another line, I think. Another. Something magnetizes calmly from my core out into the world. I leave the bathroom, knees trembling from impact, and look for the bar.

In the middle is the photographer, with an empty seat next to him and a full pint waiting there for me. I walked up to him slowly. He had shed his blue hoodie, was kind of sweaty and in a black T-shirt. He was hunched over, intently scrolling in the bar light. My stomach fell through earth, my mouth watered. Every cell of me said leave, but the prospect of more drugs and more to drink owned me entirely.

I sat beside him, feeling his pain as I crossed my legs. I took a long pull of the beer. He didn't look up, just reached his large hand to my thigh and said, I like you in a dress. I don't speak. I drink deep. I close my eyes. I hear him order me another. I saw the sea he pulled me from, all around me in blacks and blues and violets. Surging. When I blinked back into the bar, I started on the fresh pint. Do you have any more blow?

Later, it's eight a.m. and I'm slumped at the twenty-four-hour biker bar Gabriel showed me with the photographer. I remembered Gabriel being here and wanted to run into him. I called Baby and told her I was headed deeper into night, that I didn't want to but I was. She hung up. A tall guy, the photographer, and I did lines in the bathroom and touched—I closed my eyes and pretended it was just the tall guy and me. The pain of before fell as a truth so fundamental, it almost didn't exist. Or I didn't exist.

I was almost caught by the photographer again but pushed my way out of the bathroom before it was too late. I told them to kiss and they did, lazily at the bar just once to appease me. I couldn't remember the random guy's name. He was aloof like Gabriel.

The photographer asked how I could consider myself trans. You're equally invisible to me, I thought, smiling. I caught my reflection in the mirror behind the bar. My face lined with the living I chose.

I wound myself into the highest, saddest dark. They'd call me Henry fucking Miller if I was born a man. I'd be unbothered and high and drunk, striking out and writing for my projected abjection. No one but myself to know, to answer to. What an idiotic luxury, for the world to think of you as a person with things to say.

Gabriel messaged me from this bar once and told me about a dream. It was the one about me on my knees. Original sleeping life you have, I responded. The random guy next to me asked what I was doing, at the bar at eight a.m. on a Tuesday. To feel something, I said. He left.

With the photographer, I become a solitary whore. Indulgent, sullen. I get nervous about the light outside but I chug hard. I am the only power that makes me do this. My intake is getting wider, more profound. There's little space for anything else.

The other drunk men wade in their drinks. I keep looking at them as if they can do shit for me. I give the fuck up on this too-long night that is my entire life. I do more blow in the bathroom before finishing my beer and heading out with the photographer. I want to go to Gabriel's. My ache for him is vicious. We fast-walk through the graveyard. The morning streets are lush and sad and damp in cold light.

When I get to my door, the photographer hugs me and says, Until next time, passing me a vial. He's scarier in the daylight, so I don't hug him back. I shower and I get into bed with Baby. She rolls over and, with her early voice, says, I thought you were gone.

I sloshed my form so hard for so long I disintegrated into an anti-anthem. I collected the crumbles of me and got them fucked, high and deteriorating into the threshold of time.

I don't know the markings of our time because I'm still working my way back to utero, particle by particle. I want to go back and be called my name. I want to go back and then back out as a me people can see.

That afternoon, Baby went to work and told me to chill. Chill, I thought. Chill, just chill. I tried to lie there, chilling. I tried to clean. I tried to watch something, but all the chilling was stressing me out. Cuts to the photographer severed me from anything except my hot circumference of fear. Sharp, each flashback. I needed to smooth it all over, and one vial wouldn't be enough, so I called the guy and told him to come up.

When he came, we cut into the vial and had a drink together. He didn't say much but seemed comfortable. I turned up the music and asked what else he had. I asked for some ket and 2C-B, some acid and another vial of speed, agreeing to pay him back in full next week. I brushed his leg under the table, so brief it could be read as a mistake. He got my signal and looked me in the eye. We moved to the edge of the bed.

He seemed amused by me: the tab on my tongue, inhaling speed and then popping 2C-B. You're crazy. He shook his head. I played along. Yeah? You think so? We kissed, and the world fell into nothing. I had almost arrived where I'd always been getting at. I was close but I needed a drink. I took his hands off my chest and dragged him to the corner store to get something hard. The neons bled together and every outline in the world multiplied. I got two big bottles of bad whiskey and some bubble gum.

Back in the flat, it all flung out before me. I needed to lie down. The guy left. The bathroom tile was a precious cold on my cheek. I remember heaving, reaching for more whiskey. I remember the soft linen cover of Baby's pillow and reaching for Baby's voice. I sank into a total dark, the Cramps record circling.

Only a poet's voice will do. This is The Angel Natalie's. Coming here, wings long and true. Coming here, to the clunky, overdosed plea of me to tell you: There's no juice, no wild, momentous happening here. It's just the banal entertainment of death getting as close as breath. The true nothing of it all is boring and passive. My dumb flesh, churning in a black death bath of drugs.

See, The Angel Natalie's sun rises frankly, and in earnest, her light unavoidable. She says, "This is Sid and Nancy without the Sid and Nancy. No talking, no literature. Less than drama, shitting guts and heaving, passing away into black."

I got gone enough to never be back, but there are flukes. There are spectral landings and lucky departures. The wind of the Angel Natalie's wings cooled my skin and her sun cut the dark.

Gasped back into life, I woke in the hospital. I tried to reach Baby with my voice. I could smell her, lavender and paint. I wanted to sink my entire living into her, to show her the crux of me, of us, of how good I could be for her, how unlike myself I wanted to be.

I'm so sorry, I whispered, looking at the unbearable ceiling, hot tears collecting in the outside corners of my eyes. I split down the middle. I'm sorry, I'm so sorry. She just touched my forehead, got up, and opened the door. Your dad's here, she said.

You're awake—his voice filled the room. He and Baby came to the side of my bed. A nurse came in and attached another bag of liquid into my IV. She told Dad things in German and he responded with a smile. Well done, sweetheart, you didn't die. He hugged me. He sat in the lone chair and told me that he bought me a ticket to the Midwest. You'll stay with your mom. He goes on, She's agreed to help find a place for you in rehab, it will be good for you. Baby touched my hand. You'll

go to treatment, won't you? I slowly nodded. Give me a fucking second, I thought. My life is over, I thought. I'm sorry, I'm
so sorry.

Baby squeezed my hand. Dad looked kind of scared. The
stillness of the room hurt. Can you turn off the lights? I
asked, looking at the IV in my hand. My body felt weak; my
head, empty. The shame was too big for voice. Still, I tried
blinking back into life: I'm sorry.

My index and middle curled around the cold metal of the seat belt. I held them there for one, two. Then lifted. The dark tunnel full of heads, illuminated by screens, the thick stale smell of animals assembled in bite-sized, badly seasoned plastic rectangles, the sweat dripping on the thin transparent covers. I waited for the bathroom. A flight attendant was reading something thick. I asked for two more beers. She asked how many I'd had. Three, I lied. Here—she winked as if guilty and handed me two green cans. What are you reading? I asked. She looked up at me and tilted the cover to face me. It's a book where the author's name is larger than the title.

Her eyes made me hot even though she wasn't reading Bolaño like I hoped. I cracked one of the cans. A tall man left the stall. I stared at his neck and thought about burying my nose in his warm skin, then biting down. You're so fucking hard, I told myself. I entered the bathroom and looked at myself.

I missed Baby. I put down the seat cover and sat. Then I chugged. I get going. Legs wide. I push free fingers into my mouth. As the surge follows I go harder. I thought of María Font, I thought of Baby. Their dark long hair. My rain making them wet. I'm Bolaño, and Baby's legs are wrapped around me. I get there. Wide-mouthed and silent release. I smell Maria's rain and leave the bathroom.

I asked for another beer. The plane jolted and a few tears smudged what was left of the purple sparkles on my eyelids. Baby, I say to myself, Baby. My beers and I went back to the dark plane, still bobbing. I opened up *The Savage Detectives* and skipped to the scenes with Maria. I imagined her next to me, coming with me to Iowa before we got an apartment together in Roma Norte. I passed out with the book open on my lap: her legs wrapped around me.

negative one:
iowa

The plane landed in Chicago. It was night. My flight farther west took off the following evening. This gave me time to rest in Dad's apartment for a night before going all the way home, to Iowa. He wasn't in the States often. He lived all over, working like always, hard sturdy hours using his brain for technology, for future, for innovation, for money.

He called and wanted to know things that I had a hard time answering. He told me a good place to get food. He told me they had that burger that tasted like meat but wasn't. The bed is American-big. White sheets I roll-clutch as if to brace myself for the doom of living a life without Baby or Gabriel, a cruel ocean between me and everyone. Last night comes in slices: walking to a bar, any bar, angry. Alone on a massive leather couch with my good friend whiskey. The lighting is off, too bright for this interior. A guy comes and says last call. It's early. But we are in America. We are against enjoyment.

Then I'm outside with no one, looking up at the Wilco building and down to the river, blasted by tall wind. The bridge moans with me. I stand with it, maybe becoming it. I could just step off and smack into that river glimmer, that cold dark below: to sink till the dark below is the dark above.

Then I'm waking up in the apartment, getting a text from

William, my high school boyfriend, about meeting in an hour.
Fuck. I long for Baby but stop myself from calling her. The
whiskey in the freezer is Dad's, so it's good. I pour it thick
over those big perfect slow-melting cubes. I drink it too fast
to think.

I put on a dumb record I bought in Wicker Park three years
ago. Then I need food. I eat bites of it all: hummus, tortilla
chips, carrot, Valentina hot sauce, leftover cheeseburger that
I don't remember buying, olives, cheese, dark chocolate. I get
bigger with each bite, crouched in front of the wide, offensive
light of the fridge. I go from the cold wide kitchen to the wall
of windows. I look down and get dizzy.

I'm swollen but trying to ignore it. I'm massive. Obese, now,
after all that chewing and swallowing. I drink more whiskey
and pick up my pack. A cloud moves and the sun hits me as I
remember I can't smoke inside in this country. Just wanting
to hide for the rest of forever, I disable the smoke detector.

I'm in the shower now. I get to my knees. It's time, I assure
myself. It's okay. I shove my index and middle down and back
till I gag. Nothing. Should've had ice cream. I feel a surge of
arousal, the hot water on my back, on my knees. I think of
Gabriel in my throat as I press the bad food out of me. Out it
comes and down the stopless drain. And there I go, the bad of
me. It takes time to get good. My fingers prune and my knees
ache and my lower back stabs from heaving, but I've done it.
Crouched and holy in my ritual, I'm empty. I've won.

I stand up and hurt completely: it's an even oblivion to sink
into. I get light-headed and love the momentary droop. I knew
a minor faint was always a sign I didn't have any bad in me

anymore—like my sister, fainting during mass: small and perfect and dramatic onto the solid pew, incense and deep singing and red polyester.

I dry off and put lotion on my new, tiny body. I wear the jeans that Gabriel loved, the ones that are for women and are tight. They are perfect now; I can feel the space between my stomach and their waist. Good job, a voice tells me. It's the voice that loves me small like this. Usually it's telling me to hate each thing, each swallow of any food, ever. I've won this voice over, done its dirty work with elegance, with grace, so now I can move free. I can step wide, fast. Even sitting and crossing my legs is a hot and glowing calm.

I throw on a huge T-shirt and let my hair dry the way it wants. I refill the glass of whiskey, the swallow is sublime, going into all the space I've made. I make sure my bags are packed for the flight to Council Bluffs. I message William back: come to mine and bring good whiskey. He agrees and I wonder if he'll hold me down and kiss my back like he did in high school. I message Baby: landed. I miss you, are you good? I look at Gabriel's profile on Facebook, I'm still not his friend. Pushed away, I want him to see me in this hallway mirror in the jeans he got hard about, my wet hair. I take photos of myself. If only my body could drive him back to me. Below my image to Gabriel, I'd write: I'm empty, fill me up.

In the arrival's hallway, Mom's waiting in a light pink V-neck T-shirt and beige shorts. She has big sunglasses on and a thin necklace with a small, glinting stone. She let a swoop of gray grow out and the rest of her thick hair is blond. Her skin is tanned and her nails are neatly done in beige polish. A thick Claddagh ring is on her left middle finger, heart facing out. Her smile was American white and I sank into her hug, breathing in Chanel and cigarettes.

She was sad I had a layover alone like that. What were you thinking? she asked, tucking a stray hair behind my ear. Your hair is still black, she noted. I like Chicago, I reminded her, rolling my suitcase to the exit. You reek of beer, she said. I know, I said. We need to stop on the way home. Like giving in to a long argument, she said, I'm glad you're here.

Mom takes the back roads and I love her for this. She lets me smoke cigarette after cigarette even as the dusty wind slaps the smoke back in. I close my eyes as she looks at me and turns up *Astral Weeks* by Van Morrison. Sounds that hold me, that have held me since birth. In this way, Mom reminds me I'm not dead yet.

I'm heavier, less beautiful, when I'm not bringing my beloved to my lips. Mom tells me, That must be your eighteenth Budweiser today, like it matters. My swallowed reverence: I wince at our near goodbye. Mom's truck is new, slick white, bulky and broad. She's got a yellow I sticker for Iowa on the back window. The bed is deep and I tell her so, trying to make conversation. It hurts Mom to sit for too long, so we stop often.

We stop at a gas station. I step down from the truck and feel dry from behind my eyes to the hairs on my arms. In the sun, I stretch as if to pull myself apart and away, to estrange myself from the empty totality alcohol makes me. I look wide and see deteriorating single-story buildings, a lonesome horizon of soybeans, inhumanly tall light poles, slabs of concrete and too much sky to name. I close my eyes and exhale like a prayer, seeing the thick white painted lines of the highway slide by as if we're still moving.

I follow Mom into the women's and she looks nervous about it. I ignore her but am nervous too, particularly at the counter, the cashier scanning me a second too long. People think I'm one thing, then another and then the third thing they think I am confuses them and could mean I die. Years ago, Mom and I went to the grocery store and she told me she felt like she needed to protect me, with my shaved head. I wonder if that protection has postured into a fear too big to speak of.

I put two tallboys and pickle in a bag on the counter and ask for a pack of Camel Blues. Mom buys cinnamon-flavored gum and a black coffee. The cashier mentions the weather. Mom replies with a calm smile. I feel beyond the boxy, too-bright interaction but try to keep myself there. There are camouflage hats hanging sadly on a rack. There are shot glasses that have stalks of corn on them, T-shirts with rhinestones, postcards, and pickled eggs in massive jars. The orange-and-brown-tiled floor reflects back the scent of leftover cheeseburger. There's a clinking silence to the place that is dented by the swing of the door, a loud electronic bing going off at each entry, each exit. I feel permeable, wildly visible. Your daughter? he asks Mom, nudging at me. Well, yes, my son, Mom says, exhaling and placing her arm around me as I reach for the tallboys.

Mom fast-walks to the car. Wait, look, I say. She, annoyed, comes to look. Clusters of dead monarchs are stuck onto the grille of the truck, sucked in by the engine. Mom says this happens. They make me think about the sun glowing thick on the messy long green grass, lying there with grandma, monarchs mating in the shallow trees, so many, so close I heard their wings flutter on one another. Vibrational, two making one.

Later in the drive, I ached, ashamed in full volume, saying, I'm sorry, I'm sorry, I'm sorry. She said she knew. I poured another beer into a thermos. Then she said something I'd never heard: Every day, we worry you're going to die. I fell forward, let the dash catch my forehead. With profuse tears and snot all gross and real on my face, lips and thigh, I said, damp: I'm sorry, I'm sorry, I'm sorry.

She touches my back. It's in the family, she says. I lean back in my seat. Grandpa had it too. Even me. Even you? I ask. Yeah, she said as if I already knew, I was in a twelve-step program for years. I got sober when I was eighteen.

I look out the window, not knowing how to respond. Not knowing how I could be far enough gone not to know something so fundamental about her. I know it's hard, she said flatly, addiction can be contagious, but so can recovery. Look, Grandpa died, but he died sober. And me, I can be here right now for you. I finished my thermos of beer and took her extended hand across the middle console.

I woke the next morning in my childhood bed and in my childhood bedding, smelling fatty breakfast and watery coffee, confused. Seeing myself in the wide bathroom mirror, terror engulfing me. I vomit and shower. Then Mom and I eat together. She seems to love me. I crack a beer as she tells me I drank her boyfriend's last mason jar of moonshine last night. I didn't remember. I'm sorry, I said.

We walked her small dogs. I think about how this American grid urban planning is oppressive. Every walk is straight left right left right. How can my mind wander into anything at all here? There is no space for a lingering gaze, no park lawn to share beauty, joy and light. Instead of telling Mom this, we talk about the teenage trees and complain about the heat. She wants to know why I won't swim with her in the neighborhood pool. Don't have anything to swim in and my binder, Mom. She understands or pretends to.

The mid-sized houses here are all some shade of the same flat brown. The lawns are neatly kept, the sidewalks show little time, less life. Mom's duplex is in a cul-de-sac. She hung a large sacred heart of Mary on the front door. She found it online. It's gorgeous, I tell her, wanting to lay my face on a cool polleny petal of Mother Mary's lilies. Inside, there are warm lights, candles and a huge comfortable couch upholstered in red toile. It smells like fresh laundry. The carpet is the neighborhood brown and Mom hates it. I tell her it all looks great, eyeing the Celtic cross on the mantel and the huge portrait of Grandma—she wears a thick knit turtleneck and a light pink blazer over her shoulders, her glasses dangling from her left hand.

Later, sliding the blue vase of yellow wildflowers to the center of the low coffee table, she listens as I explain terms: transmasculine, transfeminine, medical transition, t, estrogen, nonbinary, cis. She's attentive, and I thank her. Rearranging her home magazines and thick hardbacks, she asks, For what?

I find out gay rehab doesn't take my insurance. The insurance stranger tells me that it would only be covered if I was previously rejected from a treatment center *for* being transgendered. You don't need to put me in the past tense, I think, I'm right here. So I spend a lot of time on the phone until a stranger doesn't say no. My Mom bakes Irish soda bread and we eat the loaf throughout the evening—cutting slices to spread with butter and lemon curd.

The next day, a place in a small town north of us says they will take me. Mom is relieved. The stranger tells me I can stay in any gendered room I want. The rooms are past tense too, I guess. The lesser of two evils, I choose a big room on the women's floor. I have to wait a week for the bed in my any-gendered room.

I spend the waiting on Mom's front steps, smoking in the insane sun, fielding glares from the neighbors. I carry a bird-bath up the hill to the garden for Mom. I lift other things too and she seems thankful. I don't dream, or think, really. I pace the perimeter of the backyard with Black Flag at full volume in my headphones. I can't die here.

Mom drives me to get beers and nicotine a couple times a day, or even in the middle of the night if I'm desperate and rude enough to wake her. She tells me, defeated, to just buy a thirty rack so we will have one less trip. I feel disgusting, hefting the huge red, white and blue cardboard-covered cans up on the counter from the handle. The cashier likes to talk. Too scared to make it past our hey-and-how's-it-going routine, I suffocate into a crushed aluminum, masculine sadness. I promise myself that these will last me till tomorrow.

I walk out of the gas station and meet Mom's eyes as I lose grip on the beers. They smack the hot pavement and roll under Mom's truck. Fuck. I rush to pick them up, the dented cylinders sweating. Mom gets out of the truck and at the same time the cashier runs out and says with a laugh, Don't worry, sir, I'll give you another one.

We drive home, laughing at the stupidity of this, of me, of her, of this disease. There is a beautiful cluster of loose fallen and dented cans by my feet and an intact cold thirty-rack heavy in my lap. Too bad you're charming, Mom says. People will always love you, no matter what you put them through. This makes me feel sick but I smile like it's a compliment, the anticipation of my beloved all around me. I'm alone and soaked in my first love, relaxed and looking out the window, unbothered by mute suburbia. Mom is strong and puts up with my permanent drunkenness. The stranger from the rehab on the phone told Mom that with how much I drink, it's not a good idea for me to detox at home.

Wait, we need to stop first and get another beer. We're not doing that and you know it. Mom pulls up a long hill into the parking lot of the dual diagnosis rehab center. It's in an old monastery where the nuns couldn't leave.

A beautiful boy with glossy eyes asks me how I am. I nod. It's strange to be so close to someone so alive. I mourn the half-drunk tallboy in the truck door's cupholder. Mom seems relieved and talks to someone who smiles and touches her shoulder while the boy makes me blow into a Breathalyzer. I fuck it up the first time because it's hard to breathe. Then he shows me orange letters that say .29. He explains, really gently, that for safety reasons I have to go detox at the local hospital, then come back.

Mom drives me. I plead for another beer before the hospital. She just laughs. This is going to be good for you. We hug long in the parking lot. She, exhausted, gets inside the truck for the three-hour drive back. I walk toward the hospital. It looks empty. I smoke and pace on the sidewalk out front. There must be a bar nearby. I could find one. A dark bar and a sweating pint made me furrow with clenched, life-saving certainty.

Everything I ever needed was in that drink. I pretended Gabriel was waiting at the bar, held the straps of my backpack, walked away from the hospital's glass façade and headed down the road to the bar, any bar. My hands twitched and I kind of stilled them by punching hard and deep in each front pocket.

I was the sole pedestrian. Some men in trucks looked my direction. They didn't scare me and I didn't need a ride. I could feel the beer grow nearer. The sun was strong. I sweated in my black cut-offs, worn Birkenstocks and white T-shirt. The houses were all weirdly-colored ranches that depressed and disgusted me in their stillness. It felt like this was the only neighborhood here. The lawns were unkempt and shallow. Where were the people of this place? I looked to my left and saw the monastery just across the street on a steep hill. There was a massive sign on the lawn in bright green that said: PROBLEM WITH ALCOHOL? Fuck, I'm already back. Small town is right. I picked up pace and walked without being seen, thinking about the living boy with the beautiful eyes.

A watery blue Bud Light sign in neon on the front window of a building led me in. I walked cool down a steep hill to my love. Behind the bar, there was a thick chunk of the Mississippi, so wide it almost became a horizon line. There lay gorgeous slabs of limestone and lush trees. There was a casino too. I was feeling causeless, and my mouth watered, navigating the raft of me to shelter.

The door wasn't locked, so in I steered. I said hello and looked for signs of the living. It smelled like grease and vodka.

Maybe they'd let me smoke in here. Then someone dead like me came out from a neon back room. I lowered my voice and sat down on a red barstool. He said they weren't open yet. I said please.

When the sun started to set, the guy like me told me to get the fuck out of there. He knew I couldn't pay. It was hard to steer now, I was thick with drinks and heat. No one had blow or a plan. Someone called me Johnny. I walked to the door, thinking about a limestone sleep on the Mississippi's bank.

When I looked up, Mom was in her truck, parked on the street across from the bar. Her window was down and she yelled for me, honking. A shame rage rose so large I couldn't breathe. Fuck. I stumbled into her truck. She looked at me, angry, but hugged me and said, Goddammit, I thought you were gone. Feeling like I understood limestone, I pulled away from her, closed my eyes and sank into the passenger's leather, feeling the light of the Mississippi.

I woke up in a yellow gown with an IV pricked on the back of my hand. The needle went right through my Ponyboy tattoo. It was in Toni's handwriting but Baby gave it to me with the photographer's tattoo gun. I spun my legs to the floor to stand, and my bed began beeping. A nurse, busied and not taking much notice, came in and scolded, You're just trying to get me into trouble, aren't you? She looked at me looking at her. She flipped a switch at the foot of the bed and the beeping stopped. You're a falling hazard, she explained.

I sweated through to the bed but was cold to my core. There was no comfortable way to lie. Every angle of me twitched in fluorescent pain. When I made it to the bathroom I saw myself and it felt like a long time since I really had. The nurse told me they had to check my vitals every hour. She stuck wires with stickers on the end to my chest. She wrapped the puffy plastic rectangle around my bicep. You don't use intravenously, do you? Huh? I asked. Beautiful skin, she said.

I shook and thought of beer. I drank lots of water and tried to vomit. Then I scrolled aimlessly on my phone screen. Then I called Mom. The rehab had called her and said I hadn't checked in at the hospital. I turned right around, she said. Her voice sounded hurt and far, far off. I asked, How did you find me? as if it really were a question. It's a small town, there are only so many bars. Mom said she came inside to grab me but there was a rage in my eyes that scared her. I don't remember seeing her. The nurse came in and my brain flashed to the bartender's forearms in the back room of the bar last night.

Mom waited there for an hour. She told me she thought I'd never come out, that she'd have to drag the insanity of me into her truck or call the police. I'm sorry I scared you, I said. I'm really sorry. Mom sounded taller as she said, You really thought you could get another run past me? Then she asked, What's the last thing you remember? Rolling over, I said, I don't remember.

Why can't I smoke in here? I smiled at the nurse. She put her thick light blue acrylic nails on her hips and said I needed to sleep. Can I have a beer? She didn't laugh. I asked her about her family. She talked about her dog, Frank. She gave me something good for sleep.

I woke in my own cold blood. All over my gown, covering the whole side of the bed. I checked all over my body, nothing. I tried to sit up in the dark to press the button to call the nurse. The little needle on the back of my palm tore loose. It was still intact, inside, under my skin, just sideways and letting out a steady flow of blood. I saw Baby's poppy-red sweatshirt on the bathroom floor, heard my heart beat loud and slow and waited for help.

The nurse was calm. She gave me a new gown. Not the falling-hazard yellow. I had graduated to green. She changed my sheets and took out the rogue needle. She told me we could put in a new IV in the morning. I eyed the Mountain-

Dew-colored IV bag with contempt. What's in that anyway?
The things you lose from drinking, she said flatly. She said
I should try to sleep, giving me a pill I hoped was Librium
in a small paper cup. The pale-yellow floor felt wrong on my
bare feet as I moved back to the once-bloody bed. I lay in gray
light. Outside the window stood a tall, windowless building.

They sent a little white bus to get me from the hospital. As I waited outside smoking, I thought about how much I, conceptually, hated cars and the distance they protract between me and the world. Like he wanted me to laugh, the guy driving told me the clients call the van the druggie buggy. I nodded at the rearview mirror as my heart beat out of my body and onto every carpeted seat, every glass window.

After going through my bag and taking my phone, razor, hand sanitizer and cologne, he said I could have some time alone.

The room was beautiful, the bathroom a beige marble. The windows were huge and arched, with silky light pink curtains. The bed was a king and the crown molding original. The carpet was a dated pastel-blue. I put my clothes away in the huge wooden armoire, cut with panels and arches. I brought twelve T-shirts, two pairs of shorts, Air Force 1s, Birkenstocks, ten pairs of underwear, a vintage pin-striped blazer, dark green leather trousers, an oversized black linen button-down and Baby's poppy-red hoodie.

I remembered a toothbrush and one of Cy Twombly's red flowers, torn from a book and folded in my pocket. I brought an empty notebook, charcoals, *The Thief's Journal* by Jean

Genet, the complete stories of Clarice Lispector and Gabriel's thick book of poems by Elizabeth Jennings.

I switched on the radio and country music played without static. It was something new. The song hit like a hopeful pop song. It didn't hold the deep swings of misery I ached for in country music. I turned the station and, after static, an abrupt car ad yelled at me. I left it on and sat at the foot of the bed and watched an ancient gingko from my second-story view.

What's your d.o.c.? What? Your drug of choice. Oh, alcohol, speed, ketamine, I said, sitting down in a plush chair at a dusty table on the veranda. The guy from the van told me this was where people smoked, so I walked out and into a group of men.

I'm Lee, second time here. He had a mischievous edge, like there was a captivating secret hidden behind his smirk. His nails were painted black, he wore a white linen button-down, red Adidas shorts and no shoes. He asked, They got you on Librium? I nodded. Lucky bastard. He shook his head and sat down across from me. What you smoke? I slid my pack of Camel Blues to him and he shook his head and said, I smoked those twenty years ago.

The two other guys said hello and told me their names. I looked up and down the long veranda. There was table after table and clusters of beautiful wooden chairs with pink satin upholstery. In the archways that looked outward, you could see the grounds: the unused, empty pool, the lawn furniture, the fountain and the rosebushes, the walkway, the shed, the brick wall keeping us in and the gingko.

I couldn't exactly hear what was happening, but I felt it. I pulled the schedule out of my pocket and saw the next thing

was probably group therapy. I don't have a watch. There
are clocks everywhere, Lee replied, pointing to one behind
me. You don't have to do anything your first couple days, he
said, most people sleep. All I could feel was beer. I thought
of my massive, empty room and told Lee I'd follow him to
the next thing.

In group therapy, I sat quietly. Some people cried, and I
hovered above my seat, feeling distantly alive and pulsing.
The boy with the beautiful eyes came to the door with a clip-
board and summoned me over. I followed him upstairs and
he asked me a lot of questions about when I started and how
long, and medications and diagnosis. Did you take the Librium from the hospital? he asked. Yeah, why? I glimmered
with the thought of him sneaking me more. You just seem
really awake, people tend to zone out, or sleep all day when
they're on that. Oh, I said, maybe you should double my dose.
Ha, good one, he said with a laugh, writing something down.

In our morning meeting the director tells everyone that I'm new and I say hello. I also say I'm trans, I tell everyone my pronouns are he/him. With relief and certainty, I say I'm an alcoholic and an addict. We all move on. The director talks to me afterward and gives me a hug. She's the kind of nice that is so big, it makes me uncomfortable. I hug her back.

Something is happening to me. A tidal ache forces me into sun. I sink into realness. I lift my chin to it. What's that warmth, what's this happening? I look people in the eye and see. I can walk anywhere and know I'm on earth. Color too. I see the greens and blues and silvers and browns of earth with vibrant, squinting capacity. They took me off the Librium, so I'm with the everything of the world. Me and the world, here, staying around with pure consistency, not slouched into death.

I sit and talk to my therapist and feel him seeing parts of me I don't know how to have, that I don't know are even there. The Goya copy in the hallway is hilarious and I stand before it laughing deep, tearing up with Lee. There are so many things in the world all the time, I say deliriously. He looks at the toddler with TERF bangs in a red suit and holds his hand out to mimic the boy's hand, holding a leather leash around the neck of a crow. Lee walks his crow down the hallway and up the stairs to his room, laughing. I watch, feeling the actual sensation of a smile—warm, soaring, and absurd. Good night—I laugh and turn to my room.

Last night, through the window across from the bed, I stayed up watching the gingko move. The moon made everything a crisp, romantic blue. I remembered Gabriel looking up at that same moon, perched on the sill of my bedroom window. I'll always know him like this. I was rearranging a bundle of fresh lilies into groups of two or three and sliding them into green beer bottles. I'd scatter them on every surface, among books and thick, drippy candles. Gabriel told me my space was inviting.

I felt Gabriel's gait across the room, heard him turn over in bed next to me. I saw his laugh. My tears were loud in my ears. Our entire future, gone. Even sadder, the time we shared felt gone too. I wasn't really there. I turn to the side and punch the pillow with my clenched fist. I remember those times leaving him alone in bed to pick up. His sweet pleas for me to stay didn't reach my heart like they do now.

I'd just blankly follow, away from love, those darker, impulsive glints of my ruling, solitary night.

I sit at one table on the lawn and three sweaty men come and sit around me. They just finished boxing. It's free time. I'm reading, but they all start to talk to me, smoking and panting at the same time. What are you reading? I tell them about Jean Genet a little bit—they seem to think he's cool. Why don't you box with us? one guy asks. Yeah, c'mon, dude, you should work out with us. I agree but feel nervous. One guy laughs with another about something I can't hear.

A guy who arrived this morning comes out to join us. We shoot the shit, and out of nowhere he asks me if it's a disease. What? I look at him. Being transgendered, is it a disease? No, I say, looking him in the eye, it's not. One of the other guys tells him to shut up. I tell him that I'll explain why it's not a disease another time, that I'm tired right now.

Jean Genet and I get up and go inside. The new guy sits where I sat and the other men lean in and talk to him. I look back and wonder what they're saying.

I see Mom in her old Ford truck. I see her pulling into her small-town high school's parking lot, dust from the country roads lingering on the truck's blue paint. She slams into a free parking spot and lights a cigarette. I imagine she's late for chemistry class. I imagine there's a shooter of vodka in her pocket and several empties rolling around the truck. I remember a photo of her, walking wide out of school in a thick denim jacket, with a book in her left arm and her smile devious and light. I briefly imagine each glinting moment of her life then, like mine, ruined with compulsive, secret burning swallows. Every cell of her overcome with thirst. I imagine how hard it must have been, to be so young and so honest. To know you have a problem at eighteen and to do something about it.

I remember the broad lawn in front of the church, years later, where Mom would go to meetings each week. Us kids played out front. We never knew exactly what our moms were up to. We'd roll down the shallow hill, eat candy and run around. These were the children I grew up with. Inside, our Moms all sat in a circle. It seemed to make vague sense that they would all be together in a space where kids couldn't go.

To Lee and only Lee, I explain where my scars will be. We're they only queers here. He asks, When will you get surgery? As soon as I can. We melt on the lawn furniture. The pool, to our left, looked nice on the website but is empty and uncovered. Weeds are breaking through the cracked cement around its perimeter. You're brave, he said, looking up at sky. Not really, I said, it's just something I need to do. Like getting sober, he says. I nod.

There's a close stillness between us. He tilts his chin up and runs his finger over a long scar on his throat. He unbuttons his light blue shirt enough to show me the stab-wound scars on his torso. These are all twelve years old, he says.

You must've really wanted to live, I said nervously. I'm glad you're here, alive I mean, I stumbled on, I'm glad you didn't kill yourself. He nods. Hey, you too, sounds like you were headed there. I take a long drag.

Lee interrupts the silence. I'm happy for the scars, ya know? They're honest. I nod and look at the grimy pool. I say, Maybe my scars will be my favorite lines. Exactly, he replies. I nod, tearing up as I finish my cig, looking at the table and thinking, "Werde der du bist," with my whole body.

Lee crosses his long legs and allows for a brief silence and then asks, Do you believe in afterlives? Reaching to the table for another cig, I smile. Isn't this life, after?

Drawing a field of narcotic poppies in charcoal, I listen. It's free time, which means I can smoke and read alone with coffee. I can nap or meet with my therapist, James. I can work out with men who tell me what to do even if I don't ask. Today, the overgrown lawn suits me. I decide not to care and lie in the shade of a thick tree. It's August-hot but the sweat makes me true.

An older guy jogs back and forth on the walking path. I wave at him. He's a sweet, loving person. In the meeting this morning, he wanted me to know I'm braver than he is because I'm not scared to be myself. I said thank you but didn't feel brave, I just felt unhidden.

James comes down the stairs and puts his hand over his head and squints my way. I keep sketching my fields of sensation. He calls to me and motions to one of the iron tables on the lawn. I slowly make my way and sit across from him. Would you prefer the veranda? I like the sun, I said, putting my sketch pad between us. How's the medication going? I think it's good, I say, leaning back to light a cig. It can make people foggy at first, he explains. I slide him my pack and he pauses before taking one.

No, I mean, I don't feel like I'm hovering. It's not

Librium-good, I joke. He looks at me as if this is a strange thing to say. My thoughts aren't sprinting anymore, I offer. I feel kind of dumb, kind of slow. Sometimes I'll lose the next word midsentence. The next word just won't be there. It felt like he had something else to say. Lithium has helped lots of clients here, he said, it's hopefully going to level things out for you.

I leaned in to ash in the gross tin can on the table. You're doing good work here, he said. You seem to be integrating well. I hope so, I said, leaning back and looking at the massive gingko at the other side of the yard. It's kind of nice to be walled in like this, I said. We both looked at the tall brick boundary extending out from either end of the monastery. People say that the nuns got buried in the walls when they died.

Lee and I looked at the preserved nun's room yesterday. It was on the top floor and you could look through a glass window and see a small bed with a brown blanket, a tiny desk with a Bible and a wooden bucket. There was a whole nun's habit hanging on the wall too. A plaque on the wall explained they weren't even allowed to look out of the windows because it would take their focus away from God. As I leaned forward to look through the glass, I felt Lee's arm on mine. I briefly touched his palm with my thumb and looked at the nun's pillow. He took my hand and smiled. There are cameras everywhere. He let his grip go and motioned us down the hallway.

I blinked back into my conversation with James and said, Jesus, the nuns couldn't even leave this place, let alone look out the window to see where they'd rot. James smiled as if what I was saying were amusing, not sad. He said, You know, you don't seem depressed to me. What? Your records say major depressive disorder, but you don't seem depressed. At that, I furrowed my brow. No one has said that before, I explained after a long pause of looking around. What about the other diagnosis? Bipolar? Well, he began, we'll see how the medications and more therapy go. You may want to get reevaluated after you've got more time.

I laughed. So you don't think I'm insane? I didn't say that. I think you did way too many drugs and drank way too much for way too long, he said, putting out his cigarette on the solid edge of the table.

If you start to feel the withdrawal symptoms again, tell someone, he said, and thanks for the smoke. I watched him walk across the lawn and up the dramatic stairs to the veranda. I brushed the hair out of my face and leaned back toward the sky. I felt damp with chance, the sweat of today could smear my poppy sketch so that the pasture moved back in time. I saw Stone Age farmers' hands on the precious red flower of tranquil absence. I open my eyes and the poppies are all there in my present, shaky charcoal lines, so I sit up and turn to a new page.

Something about Gabriel and drugs: It's not just wanting. I want it, I do, but it feels fundamental. The way I'd take so much of him. He made me a light-limbed stumble. I thought that meant free.

The withdrawal James talked about was something called post-acute withdrawal syndrome. It was just one afternoon in the thirty-day stay. We were on the lawn playing a game where we all sat in a circle and laughed at the new people who didn't get the secret, idiotic rules. I got antsy. So much so, I stood and paced a little. Lee told me to sit down and I said fuck off under my breath. James came over to me and had me sit at a table with him. My leg was bouncing with sureness: cold beer, now. I couldn't look at anyone, only the ground. If I didn't get a drink right then, I'd suffocate in rage and die.

James tried to remind me it always passes. It always passes, he said. Always. It passes. I made it inside through the dining room and rec room, past the med room and front office. I didn't know why or how, but I was leaving for that beer. I pushed the heavy entrance door open and looked at the parking lot. A resident assistant came and said to come back in. James came out too.

Lee came out and laughed at me and pushed me back inside. What, you're having your first craving? Poor Ponyboy. No, I need to go for a walk. I just need to. Shut up and have a cigarette with me on the veranda, he said. James said, Yeah, let's do that together. So I did. I followed them and smoked and couldn't think or see but waited. I wanted to go lie alone in bed, but for once I felt like that would only feel worse. After half an hour I felt more human and the beer felt less imperative. I'm glad you stayed. I looked at Lee, who brought me an off-brand diet soda and Jolly Ranchers. Thanks, I said, it was like I was gonna die if I didn't have a drink. Lee said, smiling, But you didn't.

I met James for therapy in a small oak room with thick carpets and leather armchairs. We went through a cognitive behavioral therapy exercise that required me to write about that man over me when I was fourteen and the other times after.

Do you think people attach your trans identity to this trauma? What do you mean? I asked, sinking. Do you think that those experiences shaped the way you see your gender? My heart pulsed out of my body, tears began to fall and the beginning of rage clenched. I manage to say, You think I'm trans because I was assaulted?

No, that's not what I mean, he said, but people might wonder. I messily explain that his logic assumes I'm broken. It assumes that being trans is an aberrant reaction to being victimized. It assumes that I wasn't trans before. Yes, that's what I wanted to get to, he explains, that you were trans as a child, before those events. I nod, annoyed, *Yes*, I was trans before I really knew it, but look, those things that happened to me don't have anything to do with my gender or my sexuality. They were violent crimes. Attaching it to my gender assumes that those men marked me irredeemably, you're giving them all the power, but I'm the one sitting across from you.

You're right, James says, I'm sorry. Let's start again. I tried to breathe myself into calm. Let's go back to where we began, he said calmly. I looked out the tall windows. Distant light found both of us through the patchy filter of the trees.

I tell this not because it is unique but because it happened. Everything around me told me it didn't, but it did. My first swallow at fourteen was love, a toxic mix of rum and something minty. I started and couldn't not finish. The burn making my eyes tear, making me dizzy. It coated me in the luxury of movement. I could walk into a room, could smile, could think. Alcohol saved me until it nearly ended me. And that me, was him.

The stairs creak as he sneaks out. He shimmies through the dog door, no alarm. Grabs his skateboard and hops the iron driveway fence. In his bag, a clear water bottle sloshing with small burning pours of every bottle his parents have. He twists the transparent white cap and opens his throat. He brings a cigarette to his mouth and walks up the street. He didn't know yet that people couldn't see him. He thought he was one of them.

At night, he'd forgot that they thought he was a girl. He didn't know they'd hurt him that way. He didn't know the alcohol was a bribe for their desire, which was him. It was more than once, but he had to keep skating. The alcohol, his love, constant in his dream and waking life.

No one is ever shocked, I tell Lee. We are having breakfast at a huge circular table. Yeah, everyone's done worse than you, Lee says through a mouth of cereal. See, everyone thinks they are the worst person that's ever lived. He chews. That's just as bad as thinking you're the best.

You're doing the thing again. I roll my eyes. Lee shrugs. You think it's bad you got arrested for being drunk? For a failure-to-comply charge? You think it's bad you went to jail for a night and your Mom picked you up in the morning and bought you a bagel?

Okay, I get it. I laughed, pouring myself more coffee. More people started coming in, saying good morning or not saying anything at all. Lee leaned in to whisper, You know, some people here have lost their kids, some have nearly killed someone or are already dying as they try to recover from what alcohol has done to their body. Lee, I begin, I get that you're older than me, but— Lee rolls his eyes and drops his spoon dramatically. I know enough not to continue. I get up and take my coffee outside for a smoke.

Total sum of everything: I want to live. I look at myself in the bathroom mirror. My skin is tanned from so much time outside. My arms have renewed authority and my brow is soft. I meet my own gaze. The days here are slow moment to moment but continue along quickly. I'll stay for thirty if James agrees. I'm two-thirds of the way there.

Come on, I hear Lee yell for me, we have group. I leave the bathroom and grab my notebook from the bed, dreading the emotional sludge to come. Lee and I are late and they ask us why. I was becoming a living person again, I say, sorry. No one laughs. The leader rolls her eyes.

That night, I told Lee to meet me in the chapel. He followed me to the spot I'd found. There was a balcony where the organ sat collecting dust. Behind the organ there were no cameras. I felt a jolty anticipation: I like you following me, I whispered over my shoulder. We barely fit between the organ's tarnished brass and the wall. I leaned in to kiss his neck. Lee nicely pulled away. I'm so sorry. A panel of hot wind eroded me. Look, you're young, you've got to get this thing right. I looked at him blankly. He leaned down and kissed me slowly. He put his hand on my side. I touched his neck. He started to push me against the organ but he pulled back abruptly and said, It's better that we don't, trust me. Why'd you have to kiss me, then? I whispered, annoyed but still pulsing at his touch. Because I'm sick too, he said, looking past me.

We walked down the balcony stairs, out of the chapel and to the veranda. As we had our last cigarette of the evening, I said, it worries me that you said sick. You're pathologizing our lives, our desires. He looked at me blankly.

Okay, he began, what I meant is that we both need a friend right now, not a lover. I admired the way he smoked with his middle and ring fingers. Look, we both need to be alive to be friends, and in order to be alive, we've gotta be clean. So we've gotta make that number one or we lose everything, including those beautiful currents you and I have. He pointed his finger down and waved it in the space between us. I said okay.

I looked at him with an appetite as he stood up and said, Sweet dreams. Oh fuck off, I said, smiling.

I woke early and walked the lawn. There was warm dew on the grass. My bare feet on the ground felt novel. I looked up at the gingko and began sketching it for Mom. The beautiful, fanned leaves turn yellow in autumn. Then they all fall off on the same day. This one massive shed makes the ground below a textured, golden halo. A gingko leaf dipped in gold hangs from Mom's rearview. I see my grandma Nancy, all jaundiced and swollen. She loved gingkos the most. She was dying and my sister and I stood by her. Dad said she said, "The princesses are here," but I didn't hear it. She was turning yellow like the gingko. Dad said that she didn't have to wait for anyone else, that if it was time, she could go out to the courtyard and soar.

Not having a phone felt monastic and savory. I could actually exist without the pull of an image on a screen. Books became more vivid; conversations and faces became more important. I wrote letters.

I got a letter from London. From Dad. He tells me he's going to get married to his girlfriend in Austria. He wants me to come. My sister and her girlfriend sent me small purple crystals for protection. Toni sent me a copy of *Herculine Barbin* by Foucault.

Baby writes me too. She sends little sketches and lines she found. She sends dried flower petals and lists of her snacks: chili pickle, milk chocolate, salami, baked Brie, pesto toast, pomegranate. Mom writes me the most. She sends a card every couple of days. They say sweet, short things.

I didn't think Gabriel would write but each time they came to pass out the mail, I allowed myself a brief hope that one soft white paper envelope would carry my name in his handwriting.

Interlude: Childhood Bedroom Lit with Moon and Only Moon

All my friends and lovers want to disappear, but I'm trying not to leave myself anymore. What company do I keep then but a meal I watch them eat? Meat juice drips down her chin. Her eyes vacant with vodka as I explain the flavor of animal and potato to her chewing grin. My plate remains empty white, polished, and in it I can only see myself at thirteen, macho, chugging limoncello on a skateboard one dark summer.

Always waking coming down or hanging over was my perpetual convalescence. There were two hours of every day when I felt less ill but not better and could see the world around me like Baudelaire, coming from decadent oblivion to sharp humanity as I walked to the park with a book I half read as I tried not to call the guy, grab a pint or want to die too loudly.

Looking out, I'd see kids on blue plastic scooters, parents tired because they found joy, cool swooshes of other young people, the slow amble of an elder and the handsome barber across the street, smoking. I watched them and wondered how they did it, how they lived.

I'm glad to be in the world of the living. It's hard here, but it's different than oblivion. It's all slower now, but I'm slower too. I wait and look and see. I don't miss the world around me, the oozy sunset light or the sly grace of a good joke or the blank freedom of time or the way a song smells as it blooms from the other room.

Slamming myself with drugs and alcohol meant I couldn't see even though I thought I was defining sight. My gaze was miserable up at the tree line across the yard. I was alone watching day become night. I sat on the painted floor of an American porch, drinking, smoking and just looking at the trees move. I hid in the corner of some throbbing dance floor in Berlin, waiting for something to change. Perched at my singular window in Paris, I watched the street below blur with each swallow. I read Bolaño aloud for no one.

Now I choose to be one extra breath in daily totality.

James waits for me at the door and gives me a long hug: Come back and see me anytime, he says. A couple of people walk out with me. You taught me a lot, one guy says. You too, I say, putting my suitcase in Mom's truck bed. She rolls down the window and smiles at me. The wind holds amber light, the parking lot is merely peripheral, for once. The people around me are primary. Easy fucking does it, Lee yells at me from across the parking lot. I jog over and hug him goodbye. He puts his hands on my shoulder as if to initiate a critically important moment. He says, No matter what. I smile and repeat, No matter what. I give him a long hug. Good luck, I tell him. Call, he reminds me.

Came back down that gravel country road. Iowa. Chunks and dust rolling. Turned on, nearly hard. Finally, driving alone. There's a funeral today. The road convex and concave through tilting barns, always crimson. Corn. Lots of it. And fenced-in animals.

There are lush green bluffs but only if you drive the back way. The highway, in its punishing gray expanse, is viewless and only good for leaving. In the winter, the thick clouded sky and white snowed ground blend into one immersive horizon.

Mellow died. Or was it Nick? The dog is dead and we've got to bury it. I arrive first. Go to the barn and get a shovel. Somehow, slung over my shoulder, it makes me feel like myself in a way I didn't know I could. Other people arrive and we all stand and talk in the kitchen. Grandma makes egg salad sandwiches on white fluffy bread. I eat half. I drink an Arnold Palmer. There are always several in the fridge, cold and waiting.

When it's time, I take grandma's hand. We lead. The codependent, alcoholic aggression of my family makes its way through the back seven acres. We go up the steep hill that bends into the dog cemetery. Everything grows up in green and gold. Little wavering winds and the beautiful blue veins in Grandma's spotted hands. At the base of her favorite tree, she touches a beheaded Mary, covered in dirt.

I think here is okay. Grandma's worried about digging up other long-gone dogs of the family—their graves unmarked. My uncle offers to dig. I've got it, I insist. Grandma watches me: Thank you, my only grandson, she seems to say. I love you more than anyone, I say back with each toss of crumbling earth. Then Mom's new boyfriend, late to the ceremony, stupid and sad with his whiskey grin, carries the dead dog over to the hole. Grandma opens her self-published book of poems. On the cover, there's a black-and-white landscape. A barn but mainly sky and soybeans trickling in the wind. She reads something about long mornings, friendship and the simple knowing of dogs. Grandma tosses a single yellow tulip from her garden as I sprinkle earth over the last friend she'll lose before it's her turn to go.

Mom and I eat at the diner across from St. Mary's. Dad's getting remarried. I say it slowly. She sips her coffee. She ordered toast and fried eggs and hash browns and bacon. I think about a Bloody Mary. The plates are thin ovals in gray tinted white.

Well, it's about time one of us did, Mom says dully. The tablecloth is checkered green. She asks where and to whom. In Austria, to the French actress. Mom looks at her food. Dad wanted you to know you are invited. We can go together. It could be fun. I don't think I can make it, Mom says, giving me her bacon.

We pay and weave our way out from among the tables. Outside, I light a cig, and Mom looks at me. I hand her my cig and hook my arm in hers. I reminded Mom; we'd call walking this way "Jane Austen-ing." Some Mr. Darcy, walking his mom up the stairs of the cathedral, sharing a smoke.

The door is history-heavy. The cool tile inside made me feel far away from myself. I didn't need to wander around. I'd been there several times that week. My favorite meeting is in the basement here every morning. We sit in a circle and people tell some kind of truth. One woman remembers my day count and I make coffee. Mom dips her fingers into the holy water and signs the cross. She looks at me and motions for me to do the same. It'll burn me, I whispered loudly. She rolled her eyes and flicked water at me, then led us to the free end of a pew.

The service was longer than I remembered, and I remembered them going on for years. Mom could really sing, and I held the hymn book for her. I thought about the sacraments, looking up at the marble arches, stained glass and golden Jesus on the crucifix. Sacrament is a beautiful word, I told Mom. She ignored me and listened to the homily. I eyed the confessionals. I thought the priest might be so repressed that he needed to repress others to validate his own repression. Then I thought I could be totally wrong. The cape he wore was creamy and golden. His outfit is pretty, I whispered to Mom, watching the gown move behind him and catch light as he walked to the altar.

Mom wanted me to take Communion. I said no, but I followed her to the altar. I laughed to myself, a relapse from Communion wine in a chalice before God. When it was my turn, I crossed my arms over my chest and someone in white gloves blessed me.

I came out and into a very flat place. Screaming, all the fucking time, apparently. I grew up in Iowa, the middle of America. I always felt like my form didn't rest. These unruly shapes of myself were always there before me and out of reach. Do you know Brandon? I do. He's from the Midwest too. But he didn't get out like I did. His story was the first trans narrative I knew. Some unsurfaced vision of myself was killed in silence when I watched his story. Some origin, evaporated.

Despite my self-repression, I reach forward to the euphoric swell of my dissipated self. I call him Ponyboy. Still, my foundation wants to suffocate me. My beginnings all call for silence. For me to not be. To not turn my cold hand on the knob of these sentences. I want not to lean on the threshold but to step through. I unlearn the initial silencer. With Brandon, I trace this track:

Hey Brandon,
"Excellent kisser," one of your lovers called you. Same, man. Hey, my sister went to college in Lincoln. Where you were born. Where they named you girl. Where your gravestone says girl.

You liked riding your bike to school. Often, you'd dream

while you rode. You'd dream about what it would be like to
have a breeze go up your shirt and touch nothing but flat
chest and cotton. You'd keep pedaling. You'd keep dreaming.
Three tears would fall from your furrowed, focused brow.
The abstract impossibility of such a sensation, so removed, so
perfect. I get it. Wanna go for a walk?

You got in trouble once for contesting the rigid, Catholic
hellscape of your high school. It got worse when you refused
to wear the thick plaid skirt they made your mom buy. Even
worse when you'd bind. You stopped going. Dropped out three
days before graduation. I get it. I read that your parents named
you after a beloved German shepherd but you chose Brandon.

I was born less than two hour's drive from Lincoln, in
Council Bluffs, Iowa. I was born the year after they raped and
murdered you. I mean, you'd been experiencing it since you
were young. Sexual violence and the murderous illusion of
their eyes. Those fields of pressure all around you vast, yet
sharp. Naming you exterior. What you wanted was simple,
I get it. To live in the way that makes sense to you. To wear
thick denim jackets, steps wide, chin cocked. To fuck the way
that made sense to you and does to me. But they wanted you
to reproduce, a vessel for the desire of your parents and their
parents and theirs and then theirs before.

I mean, what you wanted was simpler than what they
wanted of you. They marked you dangerous, insane, perverted
to invalidate your hand turned to their insidious expectations.
Cross your legs unless men want to shove themselves into you,
unless you're giving birth.

Brandon, I've felt it too. The explosive rejection of the

expanse you've been caged in. The Midwest. Unnamable sky.
Oceans of corn, of soybeans. We liked the expanse, I know. We
liked the quiet, wide roads. But we had to learn that there's
punishment here. There's a tingling anxiety, the consequence
of our chosen breath.

They killed your girlfriend, Lana, too, but that's known.
Less known, they also killed your friend Phillip. He was in
town to visit his girlfriend, Lana's sister, Leslie. He was Black
and twenty-two and you picked him up from the bus station
in Omaha. I read that he had recently broken his leg. Phillip's
mom said he climbed the long stairs to the Mother Cabrini
shrine in Golden, Colorado, with a new cast on his broken leg,
and his other, his prosthetic leg, carried him up every stair.
The visit with Leslie didn't go well, so he came to stay with
you and Lana in the farmhouse before getting on a bus back to
Colorado.

People pretend you were the first trans person ever killed,
Brandon, but we know this isn't true. The violence Phillip
experienced surpasses our myopic, white understanding,
Brandon. People memorialize you and erase Phillip entirely.
You and Lana are made to be the only ones, Brandon.

Brandon, you're upset, I know. They aren't telling his story.
My friend gave me a book, Brandon. It's called Black on Both
Sides. It's by C. Riley Snorton. In a chapter called "Devine's
Cut," he writes about Phillip's life—I know you'd want to read
it. Finally, to see your friend on the page, tangible and held
close.

Once, in high school, I went to a bar alone. My scalp freshly
shaved and binding. Some guy came up behind me, put his

massive hands on my shoulders and said, 'Sup, queer? He looked at me as he walked backward to his table, full of men with the same, persistent eyes. And, of course, that gaze still finds me. The only way I know how to stare back is to imagine you next to me. You, with your chin cocked, scared but smirking and ordering us another round before we fly down Dodge Street. See, I still gaze back with my breath at stake. And it's 'cause you're with me. On my way out, I whispered in that guy's ear, winking, See you later, queer.

I never met you, Brandon. But your life lingers like a fiery exponent, always in my peripheral, illuminating new shapes of myself. I learn, with you, that my wingspan is greater than the threat of death.

You like distant light, like I do, I know. In the hallway to the dimly lit basketball court. I know. I survived Catholic high school too. I rolled my skirt and kissed boys and two girls in the janitor's closet. They named me slut.

But I got to be boy by playing sports. My freshman year I was on the varsity basketball team. We went all over the Midwest to play games. I propped my knees on the plasticky brown back on the seat in front of me on the bus and slid down so I could only see sky. The captain of the team was boyishly mean to me. I remember staring at her ass a lot. Once, in an interstate tournament, we played a game in Humboldt, Nebraska. We stopped at a gas station and I slipped two tall cans of cold beer under my hoodie. Was that the gas station you worked at, Brandon? Saving for a room of your own, with a key?

Back on the bus, the captain and I gulped deep in the very back row. She put her hand on my thigh. We passed small houses on our way out of Humboldt. It was dark and there was no one on the road. I read that you moved to Humboldt and loved as yourself for a while. It didn't last too long.

Brandon, which house was it? We must have passed by.

They'd already got you once before. Those men, over you, forced their world of terror inside you. The police didn't do anything but make it worse, of course. When you left the station, you kept your head held high and let tears fall as you drove back home, windows wide.

Did we pass your house on the bus that night? I had no idea. No threads of your life to tie to the prospect of my own. I watch a video on YouTube where a couple of queers go into the white house you died in. They find a bundle of fake flowers resting wedged between pulled-up floorboards in the bedroom. I screenshot the image and hang it up above my bed.

With you, Brandon, I trace this track. With you, Brandon, I trace this track. With you, Brandon, I.

zero:

in every tense

I try at aching less. I watch the cart of drinks come down the aisle. An affirmative voice says whiskey. I take the sober chip out of my pocket and hold it between my thumb and index. I ask for water, no ice.

I brought both of the wedding outfits Mom and I found: a blue linen suit I found at a vintage store and a dress Mom bought for me. It's dark green and silky, not bad, actually. She watched me try it on, smiling. I know it's not your style, she said. I actually like wearing dresses sometimes, I explained. The green was rich and mossy. I touched down my bound chest and decided to push down the treacherous remembering of the last time I wore a dress.

The plane lands in Vienna. I take my carry-on down to the train that takes you to the center of the city in twenty minutes. At the Hauptbahnhof, I stand out front and smoke. I walk around and find the hotel and get settled in my room. I shower and try to ignore the minibar.

My sister, June, arrives from Colorado. We hug long in a language I haven't used in years. Oh, Dad got us a good room. She sets down her bag and looks out the window to Vienna. I ask, Where is Dad? She says she doesn't know. We laugh. She wants to see what I'll wear to the wedding.

She tells me about her girlfriend, how she's sad she couldn't make it.

My phone rings, and it's Dad, calling us back. He tells us a place to meet before dinner later. June takes a shower and plays Van Morrison on a small pink Bluetooth speaker she brought. I go for a short walk, smoking and looking. The cakey façades are cream, pale yellow, green, pink and sometimes blue. There are cozy, narrow turns and webs of tram wires overhead, there are statues of war criminals and composers and a horse-drawn carriage passes on the cobblestones.

When I get back into the room, June is holding all of the shooters from the minibar and two icy beers in glass bottles. Her hair is wet and she's in a gauzy white linen dress and red, glossy Birkenstocks. I'm just going to put these back down at the desk, she says, embarrassed. Oh, that's thoughtful, I say, my mouth watering.

I lie on my starchy sheets. When June comes back in she lies on her bed, facing me. It's good to see you, I tell her. She looks up from her large phone screen and smiles: It's been too long. I'm glad you're gay now, I say. She rolls her eyes and perches up on her elbow. Are you really doing okay? Dad told me about the hospital and Berlin. Yeah, I say, the rehab got me on new medications and I'm just doing it one day at a time. Rehab was really good, honestly. I'd recommend it. She nodded and looked at her phone screen. Dad told me about the lithium. My friend is a pharmacist and says it's a fascinating drug. I laugh lazily. Yeah, I guess it is. Wake me up in an hour, I say absently, rolling over into sleep.

This is where I roll over to. This is the warm patch of grass I choose. I let the waxy blades leave those marks on the backs of my thighs. It's almost evening. June and I wait in the park for Dad. There are clusters of blond people walking, lying, reading, laughing. June's reading Mary MacLane aloud. *I Await the Devil's Coming*: journals of a frustrated genius in Montana in the early 1800s. She's hot, June insists.

My eyes fade with the sun. I'm wearing a big charcoal-colored linen button-down that looks like a short dress. The skirt I wear under is June's. It's dark green, short and leather. It doesn't allow me to extend out long like I like, so my ankles are crossed as I lie. My leg hair is blond. I play the track of a loud joke but no one hears. My sneakers and socks are off. June stops reading to answer her phone. I look over at her. I close my eyes and think about being a girl people called hot. If I hated myself enough privately, I could be admired publicly.

Dad arrives as the sun is setting. He brings champagne and his fiancée. We greet and kiss cheeks and laugh. Juliette holds my gaze and tells me I look beautiful. I smile: Merci, Juliette, toi aussi. *He* looks beautiful, Dad adds. June laughs in commiseration. We all cheers, my glass full of flat, warm water.

Through the pitchy blue dark of the park, we walk to the restaurant Dad likes. The server asks me if I want wine and everyone gets still before I answer, Nein, danke. We eat. I watch the pours of wine in the big shiny glasses. The buttery, amber circles they make in the bulb before tilting back to hungry mouths. I get the sense that Dad is taking it easy at my expense, but after dinner he leads us to a secret, smoky bar behind an unmarked door.

Dad orders shots of something and hands me one. That's okay—I slide it back to him. He laughs, smiling wide. They didn't put alcohol in it, it's agave nectar, no liquor! I laugh and take my tiny cup of nectar with everyone. Juliette looks timeless, smoking on the leather couch across from June and me. When Dad gets up to talk to other men in blazers, I leave Juliette and June for the bathroom.

I can see a bottle of Diplomático behind the bar, glossily turning in my head. I try to lean against that infatuated glance. I think of Mary MacLane saying: Kind devil, deliver me. I walk into the door marked FRAU. People laugh and toast cheers behind me, then I'm in the ballady, cool tile dim of the bathroom.

In the stall I think about blow and a glass of water with a bottle of Diplomático. Gabriel surfaces, and a sinking pain drags tears. I see Baby's hands in plaster. I try to want something more than getting fucked up. I leave the stall.

This is where I stand up inside myself. Dad and Juliette and June fall away and I'm left facing the boy of me. I take him by the hand. We laugh at my stupid fucking skirt.

I walk, feeling raw, to the table. Everyone has another

round. A server fills an empty tray with the empty shots and rocks glasses on our table. June and Dad are talking loudly about football. Juliette motions that I come sit by her on the couch. I ask the server, Kann ich bitte ein Mineralwasser haben? then sit next to her. She lights me a smoke. I'm so happy you are here, she tells me like it's a secret. There have been so many things to get ready for the wedding.

Bah on peut parler en français si tu veux, I offer.

She asks, Auf Deutsche?

I shake my head no.

She exhales, takes a drink.

You know, you don't have to get married. I wink.

She looks tired but smiles like it's a sensation through her whole body. She mocks, So you can only be funny in English?

I accommodate Uncle Montana's stare. It's hot and we're all at some mansion in the countryside just north of Vienna. Dad explains flatly that one of Strauss's pianos is across from the dining room. You could play us something. Sure, I say.

Without thought, I ask the young guy working in the kitchen for three beers. I head up the back staircase, painted a penial, Grecian white. Hemlock, I think, laughing to myself. I didn't choose a perfect Athens, I chose Athens as she is, and if Athens wants to put me to death, so be it, I think, laughing to no one. Socrates was a prick and he was right. I squint and trip a little. I stash two beers behind a small tree potted in one bend of the hallway below a skylight.

I pass the master bedroom and see my soon-to-be-stepmother smoking a cigarette in a blue silk slip on the unmade bed. I walk in and nudge a beer in her direction. She says, Of course not. I say, Of course not, and keep it closed like it isn't for me. She doesn't notice and passes me an unlit cigarette. Nervous? I ask. Terrified. One of her tall, unreasonably kind actress friends pours her more champagne.

I make my way back to the kitchen. I help myself to an empty dark blue glass. I turn into the bathroom, which is painted—ceiling, wall and floor—in hot pink. I push up the wire curve and the beer's cork pops. The label of the beer is light pink and I pour it slowly into my glass. I stand back and look at myself in my girl outfit. I look vaguely present. I take down my hair and stare at the glass of cold beer before me. The dress Mom chose makes me want to die in a slow, pixelated eruption. Out of context, I feel none of my girl/boy whimsy. I feel stupid for not wearing the suit. Someone lightly knocks at the door. I pick the glass up and bring the cold, heavy vessel to my lips.

As the golden froth falls into my mouth, my brain takes one major bend into frantic, melodic movement. Before I know it's happened, I've chugged the glass, rinsed it out and asked the kitchen to fill it with water, sucking on a mint.

Dad. Where's Dad? June passes me. Have you seen Dad? No, where is he? The dock. She laughs like something is hilarious. What? Just go see him.

I walk across the yard, there are clusters of people in white, in colorful hats, in gowns. There are children and their nanny running around. There are tall cocktail tables and couches. I walk past the white chairs in rows, past the altar, down to the pond.

You're kidding me, I yell. Dad turns around. We meet at the dock's beginning and hug. We laugh, taking each other in. We are both wearing Chucks. Dad's suit is white linen and his chucks are red, not white like mine.

You're in a dress! That's weird, he says. I'm happy that he finds it strange, then I'm sad. He looks at me and asks if I'll listen to his vows. Of course, I say, of course.

I feel like doing blow. I've made my way through the stashed beers and have moved on to gin in my tonic water in a wineglass. June asks if I'm okay. Yes—I nod stiffly.

I walk past the master bedroom to stash more bottles and see Dad, who sees me and says, Come in. I feel a remote calm. Uncle Montana pours heavy inches of whiskey for the two of them. *From a Basement on a Hill* by Elliott Smith is playing at a low register. I grab Dad's blazer for him to arm into. I sit in the open bay window with Dad as he puts his red sneakers back on.

A warm wind blows on my neck. A cello and two violins from the garden float into the room and make it into a delicate landscape. Still, Dad's music from the small speaker on the dresser churns, confirms the dark center of it all. Thanks for asking me in, I tell Dad. A scope of possibility flooded me when he asked me to be there. A momentary glitch where I am allowed to exist in men's space. He nods and looks at Uncle Montana. Uncle Montana, with his dark beard and red trucker hat, walks over to Dad and pats him on the shoulder. Let me have a moment with your Dad, just us guys. He winks.

I walk downstairs to put more gin in my tonic.

The ceremony is short and makes me cry. When I'm asked to read the Mary Oliver poem Juliette asked for, I shiver at what they call me.

After they are married, we sit around tables and eat food. Uncle Montana, sitting across from me, tells me he knows someone who thinks they are trans. I say I'm trans. He says I'm okay because I don't make it his problem. I laugh and smile as he excuses himself to get another plate of food. June watches me grab his whiskey. She asks, annoyed, What are you *doing*? I want to spit in his drink and nearly do. Some other force has another plan for me, though. I knock back the drink and set the empty glass down at Uncle Montana's place. June turns to me quickly, her long, cold fingers on my arm, and goes, *Please* don't.

I wake up in the hotel room, fully dressed and alone. I vomit and shower, thinking beer. I open the mini fridge and see nothing. June comes in just as I am dressed. She passes me a huge plastic water bottle and tiny pills of activated charcoal. She sits across from me and just looks at me. I pick my wet hair up from the damp pillow and chug the water, swallow the pills. Dad is really upset with you. Something inside me falls away toward an inaccessible dark. The shame brings rattling fear. I ask June, What did I do?

She sits behind me on the bed and runs her fingers through my hair. Nothing totally awful, she seems to lie. She lets her forehead rest on my back and tells me, trying not to laugh, that I tried to fight Uncle Montana.

In the lobby I find Dad and Juliette sitting in the lounge. The bar behind them looks like the warmest place in the world. I'm so sorry, I quickly say, sitting down. I black out, I don't remember, and I'm *so* sorry. You need to learn how to shut the fuck up, Dad says calmly. I really didn't want to drink, I was doing so well, I just— You don't want to be one of those slack-jawed drunk idiots, do you? My mind scrolls for traces of the evening, memories of anything. Juliette seems uncomfortable. Juliette, I'm sorry to you too. I didn't want anything bad to happen. She smiles at me with grace and says she knows.

In Paris, I never go to the 16th but here I am. Everything inside of me wants to run away, but I walk in and sit down. The circle is big and we go around introducing ourselves. It feels shaky but good to be back in these rooms.

Smoking outside after, I meet people, I get numbers.

On the métro back to Gambetta, I close my eyes and think of Lee.

I managed to stay sober for the rest of the time in Vienna. June and I walked around together and talked for hours. Dad and Juliette seemed cautiously happy.

During my last few days there, Toni messaged me from Paris. They saw I was in Vienna from June's Facebook and wanted me to stop in Paris. They said I could stay with them as long as I helped their boyfriend renovate a small storefront he wanted to make into a record store. Is this the guy from Nantes? It was. Toni explained that they applied to a Ph.D. program at the Sorbonne. They went on, We have an extra room. It's really a closet but you can sleep there.

I told Dad. He seemed to think Paris and some work would be good for me. He let me keep the money from canceling my flexible ticket back to the States. Thank you, I said. I called Mom and she seemed nervous. I'll go to meetings, I promised. I already knew where one meeting was from the time I went years before with Baby, terrified. We left early to spend the night doing blow and drinking beer—doing what we always did.

Dad drove me to the airport. With the windows down, we rode out of Vienna alongside the light green, steep Donaukanal. I don't think I'll ever want to live in the States, I said absently. I don't blame you, he said, accelerating. Did you really want to name me Dylan? I ask. No, that was June. I wanted to name you Sam, Samantha, he said. That would've been good. I smile. He asks, You don't like Clare?

I spent some time with Grandpa Harry's poems this morning, I say. Dad brought me a copy of *The Inner Typeman*. Harry told me all about the sunrises in Iowa and his fine letterpress. I saw his callused fingertips lay each letter, each comma's cusp, each period. Dad taps his fingers on the steering wheel and tells me about how Harry rode his bike to work every morning. It starts to rain. I look forward and think of the men in my family, not for legacy but for longing. Here, Dad, listen to this one, I say.

We turn from you, fathers.
But we turn candidly.
Here no half-hearted shambling,
No mask of falseness telling you
We stare still the way you stare.
The pivot is complete.
It is not in cellars over bottled candles
We have cursed your god,
But if we blaspheme it is still standing
And within the stringent sun;
And if we rip your heart it is not with the sly stiletto
Concealed within the sleeve,
But we tear the tissue tenderly and frankly,
And our salt tears drip into the wound.

There's a long silence and Dad hums, looking at the road. I imagine him looking at me as I turn to look into Harry's gaze. With a lingering, knowing nod, Harry assures me as I veer: My grandson, the pivot is complete.

there's nothing that means more love
than page and hand
each line for sentence is
liminal horizon I
weep with

The plane lands in Paris. It's early evening. An immediate calm passes over me. The flight was wobbly. I managed not to drink and I was back, back in the place that made me.

I walk down a narrow, steep street in the 20th. To Toni's. They're outside waiting for me. My suitcase trots on the cobblestone and there's a cool breeze. A magnetic fold opens up inside of me and I start to cry. I don't know why I lived anywhere else, I tell Toni, hugging them.

I can't believe you're here. Toni smiles. Nice suit, is that linen? It looks tailored. Yeah, I say with a laugh, it is. Toni's hair is cut at their jaw and they're wearing an oversized gray T-shirt, white jeans and light pink leather sandals. You look really good, I tell them as I clumsily lift my suitcase up the winding, creaking stairs to the top floor. I say, out of breath, I didn't realize you liked Paris enough to move here. They looked back at me over their shoulder and shrugged. I briefly mourn all the drugs we won't do together, all the beers we won't drink.

Inside, I meet Val. Toni introduces me as Ponyboy, which makes me blush. Val has a shy demeanor and beautiful, strong features. The apartment is painted white except for the dark wood floors and exposed beams on the ceiling. The living room is cluttered with books, records and clothes. It smells like they are roasting vegetables, and all the windows are swung open to the street.

Toni takes me down a short hallway. The room has a small window and a single bed. It's perfect—I hug them—thank you. Toni asks how many days sober I have. I don't answer.

We eat together in the living room. I sit on the floor across from them. Apparently Toni and Val met on a dating app and then met in real life and now live together in real life. Toni asks if I'll help them with French. Val nods and winks at me like we have a secret. Bien sûr, mon amour, I say to Toni, biting into a steaming carrot.

Val offers me wine and Toni gets annoyed and says sorry on his behalf. It's okay, I assure everyone. I'm a drunk, that's all, I tell Val. Toni knows. Ask them for the stories later. Val seems amused and pours himself more.

After they've gone to bed, I slip into my/Dad's leather jacket and take Toni's keys. I spiral down the stairs and set out to wander.

I walk north on rue des Pyrénées, smirked open, my wings wide behind me.

A guy asks me for a lighter. As I stop and feel my pockets, he tells me he's always losing things. Avec des feux, c'est toujours comme ça. His mouth was a gorgeous smile as he brought a finger to his temple. I said, J'aime tes baskets. They were dirty and white. He handed the lighter back to me, inhaling deep on his cigarette, stepping back to the façade he was leaning on.

I began on my way and he called out, Tu t'appelles

comment? I said, cautiously, Comment? Ton nom! I looked back over my shoulder and thought for a second. Then I said, Je suis Eliot.

A bar was open behind him, a terrace where young people sip cold beers. His eyes were glassed and speedy, but they softened as he put his hand on his chest. Moi, je suis Charles.

Having named myself, I smiled in a way I didn't know I could, joy becoming me. Paris and Mom and June and Preciado and Dad and Baby and Iowa and Gabriel and Berlin and June and Wittig and blow and beer and Brandon and Phillip and Lee and Grandma and Mother Mary and Toni and Harry and Dora and Jean Genet and I all swell in an elated calm. With feet on ground, air in my lungs, I am unremarkable, named and known. Charles calls out as I walk away: Bonne soirée, Eliot!

To my mom for being there, for her grit, and for teaching me how to listen. To my dad for showing me the shapes of the world not as nebulous and scary but as a joke to tell, a bad dance move to make, a reason to love. To my grandma, Jean, for always writing poems. To my sister for ruthlessly believing in me.

To Misha for showing me I could live.

To every trans person here and now, and all those before.

Acknowledgments

Deep thank you to everyone who read *Ponyboy* in its various forms. Thank you for critiquing, for hearing, and for asking. To Siân Melangell Dafyyd for her calm assurance years ago that this book would be published. To Oliver Feltham for meeting my mind and challenging it. To Kate Briggs for telling me to keep going. To Ryan Ruby for taking me seriously, for his joy and genius. To Tom Drury and Amy Benfer for always being family. To Bennett Sims, Sam Chang, Liam Morrissey, and Jamel Brinkley. To Ruhi Amin for believing in me, for teaching me love. To Ekaterina Costa for her generative friendship and calm brilliance. To Larissa Fantini for their fearlessness and editorial wit. To Kylie Gava for their paintings and for always creating a sense of home. To Marcus Scott Williams, Brooke Cheney, Alice Briselden Waters, Andrea Spisto, and Max Talay for your friendship. To Steffi Schreiter for always being honest. To Keenan Kariotis for his energizing totality, his love, and his hands. To PJ Mark, Ian Bonaparte, Mo Crist, Grace Harrison and Kwaku Osei-Afrifa for their intellect, support, and care.